Joseph Converse Heywood

Antonius

A Dramatic Poem

Joseph Converse Heywood

Antonius
A Dramatic Poem

ISBN/EAN: 9783337334734

Printed in Europe, USA, Canada, Australia, Japan

Cover: Foto ©Andreas Hilbeck / pixelio.de

More available books at **www.hansebooks.com**

ANTONIUS.

A DRAMATIC POEM.

PUBLI

THE nation of all the Gauls is very much given to superstitious rites; and on that account they who are afflicted with grievous diseases, and they who are engaged in battles and dangers, either immolate human beings as victims, or vow that they will immolate them, and they employ the Druids to perform these sacrifices; for, unless a man's life be given for the life of a man, they think it impossible to propitiate the mind of the immortal gods, and they have sacrifices of that kind ordained for national purposes. . . . .

This system is thought to have been devised in Britain, and thence transferred to Gaul. And now those who wish to know it more accurately generally go thither for the sake of learning it.

JULIUS CÆSAR.

ANTONIUS.

The Sea-Shore.

ANTONIUS AND KALIPHILUS.

ANTONIUS.

Now comes Apollo from his Eastern couch,
With gleaming armor, quiver freshly filled.
At Night retreating, and her falling hosts,
Whose countless silver helms fast disappear,
He flies his golden shafts; more swift they
    sweep
Than from ten thousand arms, on northern
    plains,
Of wild barbarians rushing into battle.
The rainy Jupiter, who, in yon vale,
A love-appointment had with certain nymphs,
Which dwell hard by beneath the archèd wave,
Hath tired grown and overslept himself.
His cloudy form now rises with surprise,
Pricked from repose by mischief-loving bolts
Of his co-dweller in ethereal heights;
While, up the mountain sides, the misty robes

Of the affrighted nymphs are vanishing, —
Fleeing in fear, nor heeding where they go.

KALIPHILUS.

Which, to speak plainly, means the sun is rising,
Clouds moving up the hills, and in the vales
The noiseless lakes of fog desert their beds.

ANTONIUS.

And still the ocean, as a wearied god,
Or one who at a feast hath overstayed,
Moves restless in its sleep, and often sighs.

KALIPHILUS.

It hath worked hard —

ANTONIUS.

     Indeed, it worked itself
Into a most destructive passion, leaped
At heaven's throat, and on its haunches stood
Till it were no wonder that its back were
  broke
With writhing.

KALIPHILUS.

    Bad digestion well may cause
Its restlessness. Thou say'st its maw contains
Your entire army, engine, armor, ships?

ANTONIUS.

Nay, now thou ranklest my deep wound again.
For braver souls than those who sailed with me
Have never crossed with Charon in his boat.
Alas! my Sextus, that thou shouldst have gone
Before me! I had thought we should set sail
Together, and together on the shore
Of Hades landed. O ye gods, why still
So hard upon me!

KALIPHILUS.

           I beheld the storm
From yonder hill. The waves and clouds were
      mixed
In wrestling conflict, and 't was hard to say
Which mounted o'er the other.

ANTONIUS.

              Our ships were hurled
Against the skies like stones from catapults,
And, falling back into the engine's mouth,
Again were hurled, and so until their points
Breached wide the bastioned heavens, and let
      from thence
Long streams of fire.

KALIPHILUS.

And they o'erwhelmed your fleet.

ANTONIUS.

Nay, smote the insulting waves, and they in
    wrath
Tore us in pieces, trode us under foot.
And no cloud weeps, no sighing wind bemoans,
No darker is the shining world because
My comrades all were so untimely quenched.

KALIPHILUS.

Didst thou e'er see the world grow dark
    because
A gleaming phalanx of brave fire-flies fell
Into a stagnant pool, and there were quenched?

ANTONIUS.

Shame on thee! man is better than a fly.

KALIPHILUS.

Look from the heavens, thou shalt distinguish
    neither.
Be grateful that thou too wert not consumed,
As men are grateful oft for greatest curses ;
And thank thy gods that it was I, and not
The natives here, so found thee.

ANTONIUS.

                Wherefore ?

KALIPHILUS.

                              Fool!
Thinkest thou they would respect a Roman
    garb
Or Roman majesty, though great as thine?
The searching winds, the slot-hounds of the sun,
Could ne'er have scented out thy scattered parts
Hadst thou been rendered by the gorgèd wave
To these barbarians instead of me.

ANTONIUS.

Pray, let them have me.

KALIPHILUS.

                 Nay; with me thou art safe,
And mayest repose in peace, while over thee
The ægis of my power I shall spread.

ANTONIUS.

A stranger here, and yet a ruler?

KALIPHILUS.

                              Yea,
I govern as may he who will but make
Prince Superstition his prime minister.

ANTONIUS.

Art thou an enemy to Rome? If not,

Why sufferest thou this long sustained revolt,
By which her dear-won sovereignty is mocked?

KALIPHILUS.

With what pertains to nations and affairs '
Of state I mix not; and so keep my power
By using it where I can have no rival.

ANTONIUS.

If it were not too great offense, I 'd beg
To know the art by which thou hast this power.
For, plainly, thou art of remotest race,
And hast naught common with this people.

KALIPHILUS.

                  Yea,
I came a stranger; these barbarians
At first received me kindly, used me well.
But soon a quarrel grew, for I protected
A captive girl, of that new sect the Christians.
And when they found they could not take my
        life,
That neither fire nor water, sword nor spell,
Nor poison, nor the certain siege of hunger
Could make life's citadel capitulate,
And that I seemed to reverence their religion,
They took me for a god. Now am I called
The Great Magician.

ANTONIUS.

     Dost thou understand
The arts of divination and of magic?

KALIPHILUS.

I have some power o'er nature, and I can
Foretell by stars; make them to me unfold
Their hoarded secrets gathered from the past.

ANTONIUS.

Let me recount, I pray thee, my dark story,
And ask the practice of thy wondrous art,
That I may be resolved from all my doubts,
And wander, no more, darkly.

KALIPHILUS.

       Tell thy tale;
But see thou tell it all, and keep naught back.

ANTONIUS.

I am Antonius, a soldier, one —

KALIPHILUS.

Of whom the world hath heard. I honor thee,
And so have entertained thee.

ANTONIUS.

       I am one

Who, thirty years ago, stood on the mount
Of manhood's youthful prime, and smiling saw
Life brightening before him, as the morn,
In spring, beholds the blooming, brightening
    world,
Conscious of will; assured of manly power;
Elated with intoxicating draughts
From full existence's overflowing cup,
Held to my lips by all the crowding hours;
Entranced by Hope's embraces, whose bright
    train
Of promises me, each in turn, caressed,
And, in the stolen livery of Truth,
Passed, with her, to my heart, unchallenged;
    lapped
In wealth of strong affections, squandered not,
The halo of a glorious ancestry
Encircled me. I had no need to love,
To place my gems of happiness at stake
Upon a woman's gilded pledge of love,
Yet did I it and lost, for she was false.

KALIPHILUS.

Or poor, mayhap: not all the world are rich
In love and truth; few know how poor they
    are.

ANTONIUS.

Then was she false to falsely promise it,
And take from me my faith and treasures all,
For she robbed me of faith — a great loss, sir.
Some twenty times the planets all have made
Their annual pilgrimage unto the throne
Which orders all their goings, since I learned
How penniless this robbery had made me,
And I have never yet been rich again.

KALIPHILUS.

But, like a pillaged miser, hast esteemed
As robbers all her sex.

ANTONIUS.

          With naught to lose,
Through fear of pillage have been miserable.
While she was mine, or I believed her mine,
I was more proud than any Eastern king,
And could not feel myself how great I was
In having such possessions. She so fair,
So perfect in proportions, mind, and form;
A wit so rich, distilling like the dew,
Not, like the hail-storm, cutting, — 't was to me
As all of beauty had one mouth, that mouth
Were mine alone to kiss, the constant source
Of sweet intoxication; but two arms,
And it were only mine to rest in them;

One bosom, mine alone, mine isles of bliss;
One soul, where only I could bathe mine own.
O madness! that I should have lived to learn
That beauty hath a hundred thousand mouths.
Each mouth a wilderness of kisses, where
The most adventurous shall pluck the most.

KALIPHILUS.

What! can so little learning make thee mad?
Thou, from the thorny scrub, experience,
With lacerated hands hast wisdom gathered,
But countest not thy gains. Go on, go on,
Speak all the truth, and say thy beauty hath
More arms than old Briareus, and more strength
To clasp a thousand loves; more secret doors
Unto the alabaster temple domes
Upon thine isles of bliss, than starry gates
Which lead to heaven, on your Olympus.

ANTONIUS.

Ah!
The realm of ignorance alone is heaven.

KALIPHILUS.

Once had I such a love for woman, yet
'T was not so much a love of woman as
The love of beauty which in her I saw,
Beholding from a distance, while a youth.

ANTONIUS.

Still in the dreariness before me one
Great hope allured me on. I had a child,
A daughter, upon whom my thoughts were
    fixed.
By day; by night; upon the march; at rest;
In battle's fiercest storm; in my lone tent;
On mountain summits; in the deepest valleys;
Lying upon the singing streamlet's banks,
Or fording torrents; in sweet summer shade,
Or scaling battlements of frozen snow
O'er which beleaguered winds fought fiercely;
    on
The storm-tossed trireme, or asleep upon
The earth's firm bosom; still I thought of her.
At length a yearning strong to see my child
Had overcome the fear I felt to meet
Her mother — ay, I was afraid, although
Thy smile appears to say thou hast a doubt;
I dared not meet her who 'd so wounded me.
And yet, I think I so did love my child
Because it was her child — I cannot tell.
I am an old man now, and somewhat broken.
But I so loved her —

KALIPHILUS.

    Her, who had been false!

My own child's mother — fifty thousand times
As false had not destroyed my love, nor chilled
My tenderness. O I so pitied her
That she was false! I thought I hated her,
But could not do it, no, nor yet detest :
'T is true I could not.

KALIPHILUS.

         She had drawn thy spirit,
As cats the breath of infants when asleep,
While lying on thy breast.

ANTONIUS.

         Perchance it was so.
The burning sun of middle age hath chased
The mists which spread a dimness o'er youth's
      morn
And all things magnified ; and in the rays,
Aslant from the mid-west of life, I see,
With clearer vision looking towards its east,
The founts, and rills, and torrent beds of passion,
Than when beneath the morning rays I stood
Where they were springing. Torrent beds are
      dry,
The rills of fancy all have changed their course,
The founts of love, perennial, flow on.

KALIPHILUS.

Her child was to thee as her better part —

ANTONIUS.

Embodied in a glorious form, as gold
In shapes of beauty wrought, when separate
From basest ore in which 't was born.

KALIPHILUS.

            This child —
Wouldst thou its horoscope ?

ANTONIUS.

           My tale is long;
I fear it wearies thee ?

KALIPHILUS.

          For me 't is rest.

ANTONIUS.

I weary not to speak of them ; I 'm old,
And talk of what has been, not what 's to be.

KALIPHILUS.

Ah ! I would learn that; it shall be my trade.

ANTONIUS.

I am no longer here ; I do not stand

A shipwrecked man upon a desert shore,
But in a garden, where the sweetest flowers
Of Italy are blooming; from the sea
Soft breezes whisper of the cooling shades
In grottoes fair with nymphs; or where they
      walk
In coral groves; the sun hath bent his head
Until his flushed face almost rests upon
The downy pillows which the ocean holds
In her broad lap for him; I am within
An arbor; vines enlace it; roses stand,
And, bending, offer nosegays; by my side
A beauteous creation, like a woman,
But so much fairer than all women are
I will not call her woman; on my breast
Her head is resting; round her form my arm;
Her hair hath partly fallen down, and strives
To spread itself, a shadow, on her neck,
And nestle in her bosom; in her eyes
I look; we do not speak; our little child,
Upon my knee, tries to form words, like us
In vain, to express its meaning; but still talks,
Pulls at its mother's hair, and claps its hands,
And laughs.   The more than goddess by my
      side —
She was my wife; that garden scene the last
We ever played together, save but two,
For then I said farewell to her, and went
To join my legions.

KALIPHILUS.

  And those other scenes?

ANTONIUS.

Alas! speak not of them; I 'll go no more
In that direction; it is hedged with horror.
The temper of my mind, with heat and cold
Of a much varied and adventurous life,
Hath been so softened that its edge is lost.
I cannot thrust with it; it bends aside,
As sword untempered on a wooden shield.
I turned my face toward Rome, and braced
  me up,
As for rough weather seamen trim their ships.
For I expected presently to fall
Into a cross-sea, and there to be tossed
By tides, from every quarter of my heart,
In counter-currents meeting.

KALIPHILUS.

    Well, thy child —

ANTONIUS.

Now mark, how all our blooming plans grow
  pale
And vanish in the breath of Destiny:
Upon whose locks the stars are fixed and borne
In their unswerving courses as she moves

With unrelenting step ; her face is veiled
By the impenetrable blue of heaven ;
Her form concealed by thick, air-colored clouds;
Her sandals are of darkness, and are bound
With lightning cords ; her footfall noiseless as
The step of Night ; great Silence goes before.
She comes from that vast region far beyond
The eastern verge of the horizon's bourne,
Beyond the rising sun, where, day by day,
Night after night is born ; where ghostly forms
Of unsubstantial worlds, like shadows, move,
And wait, in silent patience, to be real
And join the long procession of the planets.
She passes through the waste of human life,
And goes beyond the setting sun, beyond
The sapphire gates which open in the west,
Beyond imagination's utmost goal,
Or farthest stroke of the far-reaching thought,
And keeps that way forever. In her train,
Chained by her will, and in their courses fixed
As are the stars, the gods obedient move,
Without volition do her purposes,
Yet seem omnipotent. 'T was her decree
That, tarrying at Jerusalem one night,
And staying from a feast because my mood
Was sad, and better I loved converse with
A brave and faithful friend, I should, as 't were,
Let my child pass before me, and not know

That it was she till farther she had gone
Than reach of vision, voice, or outstretched arms
Of swift pursuing Love, and so I lost her.

KALIPHILUS.

How lost her?

ANTONIUS.

How? In that I found her not.
Had I been at the feast, I should have seen
Her and her mother, — my despair and hope,
My bane and antidote, my ill and good,
The misery and happiness of life.
Or had I by a storm been less enticed, —
A proud, imperious beauty, in whose train
Walked Darkness, bearing up her heavy robes;
And earthquakes went before her to prepare
A highway for her progress; while her brow
With flaming coronets of fire flashed, —
An amorous storm, whose heavy lids, upraised
But for one moment, with the lambent light
Of swift, deep-burning passion lit the heavens,
The dull earth melted, dazzled all the stars,
So that they shut their eyes. With mighty
        arms,
The north and west winds, she encompassed me,
Played with my hair, and kissed away my
        breath,

And plucked the growing words upon my lips,
Ere they could ripen, though a tropic heat
Impelled them; held me panting, so enwrapt
With joy of being thus caressed by beauty,
That I forgot all sadness, all desires,
All wishes, hopes, and great determinations,
And, to enjoy the sweet delirium,
Like loving Antony in Egypt's arms,
I dallied in her lap, and lost my world.
That beauteous storm was but a deep-drawn
     sigh
Of Destiny, who's ever sad; that sigh
Detained me from my child, and so I lost her.

KALIPHILUS.

How lost her?

ANTONIUS.

        She conveyed herself away,
Or she was hid. In vain I sought her; none
Could tell her dwelling-place.

KALIPHILUS.

        Where didst thou seek?

ANTONIUS.

From where the glowing Orient pearls are
     twined

By gentle Night on golden locks of Morn,
While he still sleeps in her enamored arms,
To where the evening-star stands sentinel
With amber shield and zenith-reaching sword,
And further westward will not let me pass.
From where in frozen crystals, underneath
The pole-star, deep imbedded rainbows lie;
Where in the voiceless cold of winter nights
Pale, airy conflagrations sweep the sky,
The ghosts of fires which, living, fed on worlds,
Or flapped their flaring wings and slow de-
    voured,
As vultures on the chained Prometheus fed,
The bowels of some groaning mountain bound
Upon the Earth's extremest outward verge,
To where, with feet on Afric's either shore,
Old Atlas, sighing, still upholds the heavens.

KALIPHILUS.

And found her not?

ANTONIUS.

       Ay, found her not. Ah me!
From Alps to Himalaya, through the snows
Of Caucasus to Ind, I 've sought my child;
From where the waves of storm-engendering
    space
Break black and ceaselessly in awful silence

Upon the world's remotest promontory,
To where in busy marts man jostles man,
And many tongues meet in a wordy strife.
And now I think she 's dead.

KALIPHILUS.

      Hast thou heard naught?

ANTONIUS.

One who was dear to her received a message,
But it was worn and indistinct, and seemed
A mockery. In my dreams I 've been told
That she was dead and waiting now for me
In the Elysian Fields. And yet I feel
A strange assurance that I still shall see
My child, shall fold her in my arms, shall hear
And bless. 'T is not belief, nor thought, nor
      hope,
But a small voice within.

KALIPHILUS.

          'T is hard to undo
The grasp which clings to a last hope on earth;
And when that hope is gone its memory stays,
A kind of image of itself, at which
We 're clutching ever.

ANTONIUS.

It is hard, indeed.
And now, I pray thee, exercise thy skill,
And so inform me if my daughter live,
And if I yet shall see her.

KALIPHILUS.

If so be
The spirits which keep locked the fate of men
Shall be propitious, thou shalt be resolved.
But, first, impart what was thy daughter's
    name ?

ANTONIUS.

Salome.

KALIPHILUS.

'T is the same !

ANTONIUS.

What say'st thou ?

KALIPHILUS.

Naught ;
I spake not. Tell me what her age ?

ANTONIUS.

Alas !

She would be very old, if all her years
Were each a dreary century, like mine.
Now, let me see: if she be living still,
She should have reached her early summer
    time,
And be as rich in beauty as is June.
Employ the powers of nature. Answer me.

KALIPHILUS.

'T is well. I 'll use my art, and presently
Will summon my familiar. Rest awhile,
Until I call thee Sleep thy cares beguile;
Within my tent a couch for thee is spread,
There gentle dreams shall soothe thy troubled
    head.   [*Exit Antonius.*
Employ the powers of nature! So I will;
Lead them with more than necromantic skill, —
The deep affections, weaknesses, and fears,
Strong man's strong passions, woman's stronger
    tears.
The tedious fool! — Good maxims well requite
If well observed, in spite of Dullness's spite;
Hear each man's story, keep thine own con-
    cealed;
So better profit by what 's so revealed.

The Mouth of a Cave.

ALPINDARGO AND SALOME.

SALOME.

THOU seemest troubled by my presence.

ALPINDARGO.

Nay,

My child, thou comest to me as the ray
Of morning, which uplifteth from the waves
The heavy darkness.

SALOME.

Is it well with thee?

ALPINDARGO.

Well as life may be to an aged man
Whose vision pierceth dully through the veil
That hides the future, and perceiveth there
Forms indistinct and dread of coming woes.
And art thou happy?

SALOME.

As a captive may be.

ALPINDARGO.

Thy heart is pure ; according to thy faith
Thou art most religious: hast thou felt no
    fear ?
Hath no foreboding shadow crossed thy vision ?
No dream perturbed thy sleep, foretelling sor-
    row ?
No revelation of what is to be
Made all thy flesh shrink, and thy hair upright
Stand shuddering ?

SALOME.

       My dreams are all of peace,
And rest, and happiness to come.

ALPINDARGO.

                'T is strange !
And thou art hopeful ? Naught hath troubled
    thee ?

SALOME.

Why askest thou ?

ALPINDARGO.

         I had a dream last night.
As in my youth I hunted on the hills
To find a victim for the sacrifice ;
A white doe crossed my path, I drew my bow
And pierced her to the heart. I lifted her,

And held — thee in my arms — thee, as thou
    art,
Thy warm blood gushing o'er my trembling
    hands ;
And, as thine eye reproached me, I awoke.

SALOME.

And that hath made thee sad ?

ALPINDARGO.

                For it bodes ill
To thee.

SALOME.

      No ill can come to me unless
My heavenly Father will ; then 't is no ill.

ALPINDARGO.

A brave faith hast thou, daughter.   After that,
As I sat pondering, a vision came :
A part thereof was bright, a part most dark.

SALOME.

Chase then the dark away, and keep the bright :
I came to say Good-day ; if thou art sad
'T will make of good day night ; I 'll go away.
Nay, nay, thou must be cheerful if I stay.

ALPINDARGO.

Rest, child, with me. I 'll tell thee what I saw.
The night was bending from the east to place
Upon its cradle in the western waves
The young moon wrapped in scarlet, which till
    then
Upon her star-decked bosom she had borne;
And lifting up herself her mantle fell,
Deep darkness, on the earth; the forest shud-
    dered;
From the far valleys voices low complained,
Like distant streams in autumn; in their beds
Brooks turned themselves and moaned; a sob-
    bing blast
Went through the wood and hurried on alone.
The waves stood back and came not near the
    shore,
And hushed their voices. From the southern
    sea,
Like drifting ship on fire when fogs are thick,
A misty form moved slowly and approached.
I knew my father's ghost: his eyes were like
Two moons seen dimly through dull autumn
    clouds;
His head was bowed upon his breast; his hand
Stretched over me; his voice was as the sound
Of wind slow moving through a distant pine.
Fast from his eyes and down his cloudy beard

Tears fell like showers about a mountain's brow.
Three times he heaved a sigh; three times essayed
To speak. At length with hollow voice he said:
I seek again my native groves to say
A last farewell. He paused. The trees all sobbed.
He slowly pointed southward, once more spake:
The death-storm rises from the distant waves;
It comes; its skirts are red with blood; behold!
From its dark bosom gleaming coals of fire
Like meteors fall; it passeth o'er the isle;
Descends upon it; lo! the groves are burning!
The smoke is black; upon it rise the ghosts
Of Alpindargo's children. Come away.
He said, and slowly faded from my sight,
While yet I gazed on him, as morning mists
Move up the mountain side.

SALOME.

                            'T was passing strange!
How dost thou understand it?

ALPINDARGO.

                            That the time
Of my departure 's near; and this is bright:
That heavy sorrows threaten all I love;

This very dark. Some great calamity
O'erhangs my people; and thou too must suffer.

SALOME.

Perchance it was a dream; ghosts come not
    back.

ALPINDARGO.

Hush! speak not so. They come to us as
    dreams,
To say what shall be, or to make us know
How, on some distant shore, they 've left their
    bodies.   ￬

SALOME.

Believest thou that dreams are visitants
From realms of knowledge where no mortal
    dwells, —
Come secretly its secrets to impart?

ALPINDARGO.

Sleep is half death; the ghost half leaves the
    body;
Half riseth to its cloudy dwelling-place;
Half looks into the Halls where future acts
Are formed; half sees them half prepared,
    half hid,
And mixed confusedly; and then reports
Distinctly indistinctness when we wake;
That is, when the half-absent ghost comes back:

So half reveals to us what is to be,
And what. is so revealed we call a dream.

SALOME.

But these are fancies, father: heed them not.

ALPINDARGO.

Respect an old man's faith. Thou hast thine
    own;
Leave me to mine.

SALOME

Nay, be not stern; I meant —

ALPINDARGO.

There! there! forgive me. I would not be
    stern
With thee. I hear the moaning autumn wind.
The gale is rising which shall lay my trunk
Broken and branchless on a dreary shore.

SALOME.

Can I not cheer thee?

ALPINDARGO.

If thou wouldst, find means
This day to place thyself beyond the reach
Of such a gale. Why should thy summer leaves

Be strewn like sear and crisp which hang on
    me ?
Thy blooming branches crushed, thy striking
    roots
Uptorn like mine, which loosen now their grasp?

SALOME.

I will not go away and leave thee here,
My kind protector and indulgent friend.
I could not, if I would, escape ; 't were vain
To try.

ALPINDARGO.

    It is, alas ! too true.

SALOME.

                'T were folly,
For we should court the dangers which we fear.

ALPINDARGO.

And I am powerless against the gods.
Let 's hope. Perchance we may appease them
    yet.
I shall proclaim a solemn convocation,
And there we shall debate the means to avert
The impending woe.

SALOME.

           Oh seek, with me, the aid
Of Him who only ruleth in the heavens.

ALPINDARGO.

Nay, I beseech thee, rouse not more the wrath
Of Britons' gods by thine impiety.

SALOME.

Forgive me — let me plead with thee —

ALPINDARGO.

What, now!
When terrors muster on the horizon, all
The winds are whispering of death?

SALOME.

Alas!
Wilt thou not learn from me to fear that death
Which dies not —

ALPINDARGO.

Eh! Thou 'dst teach me to fear death?
And make a coward of me? Fie! no more.
Help me to don my robe; and now — what!
        tears?
Ah! foolish girl! Another time I 'll hear.
To - morrow thou shalt come and sing thy
        hymns —
I like thy hymns; and when thou singest them
At twilight, and the silent stars come forth
And stand without their tents to listen, then

I could myself almost become a Christian;
But that I am too old.   Farewell!

SALOME.

Farewell!

ALPINDARGO.

What! going thus?   Come back and kiss the
      old man;
Forgive him; so, if we should meet no more,
Know that my choicest blessings go with thee.

SALOME.

Oh that I could persuade thee—

ALPINDARGO.

Well, thou shalt,
Perchance, another time.   Go now.

SALOME.

Farewell!

THEUDAS.

WHAT will my master? what new plot? what
    craft?
Who shall be duped? Now must I run, leap,
    fly —
Fly like a tortoise — my humped-back, bent legs
Unequal; head, without a neck, set fast
Upon my breast, — I, who should creep, must
    run.
A fine fat toad had hobbled from his den,
And at its mouth, in meditative mood,
Was dreaming of the goods he had enjoyed.
Ere I could gulp the bloated epicure,
As death shall snatch his man-like, beastlier
    mates,
This tyrant master ordered me away,
My mouth aflood with thoughts of coming
    sweets.
With serpents I would bind him, fast asleep,
And fill his mouth with poisonous creeping
    things,

So that he might not smite nor curse at me,
Nor burn me howling, blister me with words,
But that he 'd find a free way to revenge.
I 'll learn that way from him.   Now must I go
Prepare for use the devil's apparatus,
With which he made Caractacus believe
He saw the ghosts led from the nether world.
Ha, ha! it was well done; the images
Were truly ghostlike — ghostlike truly lied;
Appeared and vanished, moved disconsolate,
And sighed, and uttered hollow voices: ah!
Each separate hair stood up to look, with
          wonder.
My knees against each other knocked applause,
So that my master said I was afraid.
Now, though I think my master is a devil, —
Think! faugh! I 'm sure of that, — yet there
          are things
Which he knows not, and one of them is fear;
So thought my points of admiration were
The characters of fear, — which, if I know,
I 'm wiser than the devil; yet he 's wise.
He hath a wit is pleasing, and the tricks
He puts upon the unsuspecting world
Would make the burning arch fiend laugh to
          tears.
He goes this night; I must away with him,
For, if I stay, these savage British furies

Incontinent will roast me : so, with them,
I 'm sure of real and present hell ; from the
    other
I may perchance escape. Yet were all true
Which Pagan, Jew, and Christian each assert
Of Tartarus, Gehenna, Hades, Hell,
Of birth in doom, and pre-decreed damnation,
My master devil alone could lead me clear
Of stumbling into one or other of them.
So still I 'll wander with this subtle guide,
And thus absent myself long as I may
From that hot dwelling-place. Besides, ha, ha!
A feeling prompts me still to follow him
Who saved my life when those accursed soldiers,
Because my tongue was sharp, and I ill shaped,
Would slay me, though he make of me his slave,
And for such purpose saved to torture me —

Enter KALIPHILUS.

KALIPHILUS.

I 'll make her wed me — lingerest thou still
    here ?
Begone ! Obey my orders ere I burn
Thy marrow with hot pains, and rack thy brain
With aches, and put upon thee —

THEUDAS.

                Ah ! I fly.

Exit THEUDAS.

KALIPHILUS.

I 'll make her wed me; then her duty shall
Teach her to love me; though to me 't were
    one
Unwed or wed. It is her love I need,
And not its empty, desecrated forms,
To mock me and repel. Nor would I take
The counterfeited currency of love
Though duty offered it on bended knee,
To pay its tribute and discharge its bonds.
If I my purpose compass, my reward
Shall dear oblivion be of lengthy labor.

Enter BERNICE.

Ah! sweet Bernice, haste thee to Salome,
And with fresh arguments assail her soul.

BERNICE.

Alas! she will not yield.

KALIPHILUS.

                She shall — she must.
Go, let thy tongue with such hot potency
Of well selected phrases overflow
As shall not fail to melt her scruples; go,
And let thy speech be tuned to pleading tones,
Thy sense addressed by earnest action, truth
Seem springing from thine eyes into her own;
Ay, let it seem so; spread before her mind

Such pictures as, upon her ready brain,
Shall make a double impress, what they are,
And what they apt conceal. Put in her heart
Hot meanings masked in words of aspect cold,
And let them kindle there the undergrowth
Luxuriant of sense, whose growing heat
Shall still be thought but purest warmth of love.

BERNICE.

It were in vain, so simply pure her soul,
From which the weeds that blossom impure
    thoughts
Have all been plucked, or never there have
    grown.

KALIPHILUS.

Then plant them, dolt, if else they will not
    grow, —
And yet the devil himself should almost weep
To see so bright a creature tarnished; no.
Speak gently to her, urgingly, but purely,
Else our artillery shall back be thrown
To wound ourselves.

BERNICE.

                    If I her slow consent
Shall bring thee, shall I surely gather then
The tempting fruit of thy rich promises?

KALIPHILUS.

Ay, surely, as I 've promised thee.

BERNICE.

Shall I,
Permitted to depart alone, go search,
Among my kindred, what I ne'er have found
With thee ?

KALIPHILUS.

And that is ?

BERNICE.

Peace.

KALIPHILUS.

Nay, thou shalt go
Convoyed in safety.

BERNICE.

By what guard ?

KALIPHILUS.

Myself.

BERNICE.

And think'st thou I would go so ? O thou
devil !

KALIPHILUS.

Ha, ha !

BERNICE.

What ! wilt thou mock me ? Ay, thou canst.
I have no covering against thy thrusts,
But torn, and bruised, and sore with misery,
The finger, lifted, wounds and makes me shrink.
But thou art armed in proof —

KALIPHILUS.

       With honor — eh ?

BERNICE.

With curses, monster. Faugh ! I could not
  add
One drop to the great surging sea of woe
Which wracks thee wallowing. Oh if I could
I 'd throw it in, though all my life-blood went
To make that drop.

KALIPHILUS.

       A jewel that would be
Worth sounding many seas of woe for — eh ?
Pray, throw it me.

BERNICE.

     Yet have I pitied thee
Till all the quick pulsations of my heart
Were sounds of dropping tears ; have loved
  thee so, —

Ay, loved thee, — laugh, now, laugh! What!
     seest thou not
Somewhat to sneer at when I tell thee so?
Have loved thee, followed thee, left all for thee,
Made thee my god, and sacrificed to thee
All those dear jewels which that casket holds
We call a woman —

KALIPHILUS.

So? What art thou now?

BERNICE.

A thing, a useless thing, a poisoned thing,
A thing decaying, ah! a hopeless thing.

KALIPHILUS.

But find a way to win for me Salome,
And none shall be so hopeful as thyself.
Ah! be not jealous, since thou knowest well
She could not love one hateful as myself.

BERNICE.

She doth not know thee; she begins to waver,
To plan how she may win thee to her faith,
And to repent — what say I?

KALIPHILUS.

Ah! go on!

I pray thee now go on; thy words begin
To sound like music, though thy voice be sharp.

BERNICE.

Oh, she shall hate thee —

KALIPHILUS.

                 Now a discord comes.

BERNICE.

Detest —

KALIPHILUS.

    Not through thine offices.

BERNICE.

                      She shall.
Thou canst but kill.

KALIPHILUS.

     Why, that would bless thee.   No;
I 'll make thee live; and she — ay, she shall
    wed me.

BERNICE.

Hast thou no pity?   Is that fountain dry?
Dwells naught within thee but consuming fire
Of selfishness?

KALIPHILUS.

     I think there are some leaves
Unwithered yet on Memory's rank tree.

BERNICE.

Rememberest thou the days when first I loved
    thee?

KALIPHILUS.

When thou, with kisses overladen, as
A tree with luscious fruit inclined, didst bend
Into mine arms?

BERNICE.

            Accursed be the hour.
And may its swift successors each in turn
Bring to thy soul the pangs mine now endures;
Each be to thee as my whole life to me.
Did not I say to thee be generous,
And tempt me not to my undoing? Oh,
Be generous, and ask no more than goes
Locked arm in arm with purity; such love
Will bless us. Did I not say this? And thou,
What saidest thou?

KALIPHILUS.

           Love consecrateth all things.
That I would not from Paradise be driven
By the angel in thee with his flaming sword
Of purity. I said it. Well?

BERNICE.

              Thou didst,
And promised me to love me always. Oh!

KALIPHILUS.

But promise given by duress of passion
Is never binding.

BERNICE.

        Would the fiends could teach
Me how to call thee, O thou sneering demon!
Thy promises have aye been fair, alas!
Like coverings soft spread over horrid caves,
Deep into which those resting on them fall.
An angel bright asked me to lie upon
A bed of roses, arguing sweet rest;
And I, poor dupe, but felt it part, and fell
Into the mouth of dark and dreadful Hades.
Oh, think how I have loved thee; be more
       gentle.

KALIPHILUS.

I love thee, foolish girl; am gentle still.
If I may win Salome, I shall be,
As I have shown to thee, in full discourse,
King of the Jews and Christians, and o'erthrow
The Roman power in Palestine.

BERNICE.

        And I?

KALIPHILUS.

Shalt be the best loved mistress of my heart,

4

So rule my crowned queen.   Think'st thou I
    love
Salome ?

BERNICE.

      Ay, she hath so sweet a wit,
A heart so rich, a beauty so excelling.

KALIPHILUS.

I love her not, and but for cause of state
Would ne'er have wooed her.   We, whose
    hearts are filled
With love of country, on that altar burn
All selfishness and self-aggrandizement.

BERNICE.

Thou really lov'st her not, and I shall be
Loved as I once was, if she wed thee ?

KALIPHILUS.

                  Yea.

What shall I swear by ?

BERNICE.

      Swear ! Oh, do not swear;
Thine oaths have all been broken ; but thy word
Unsworn may bear the burden of my hopes.
I go, and what I can I will for thee.

[*Exit* BERNICE.

KALIPHILUS.

Fool! loving dupe! again to trust in me.
Oh how I lie! Accursed remembrance hence!
Oh could I practice devil-breeding sin,
Each vile deed, for me, live but at its birth,
No memory to set on me Remorse,
So hunting and tormenting me forever!
Let me in hot Gehenna fast be chained,
And there be spitted on a tongue of flame,
And, writhing, hang the mark for thunderbolts,
And every moment shot at with the shafts
From their red quivers, thrusting every fold
Of my contortions, till into the abyss,
Divided in a thousand parts, I fall,
Each separate part instinct with tenfold life,
And rich capacity for agony;
I 'd deem myself most happy, if the light
Of this accusing memory in the dark
Of that perdition might be all snuffed out.
Then should I be as I had never been,
And all this tide of horrors from the past
Cease rolling on me — Tut! 't is idle! what!
Shall I cry mercy to my great Tormentor?
Time presses, and my plans delay: to work!
What, ho! Antonius! awake! come forth.

Enter ANTONIUS *from the tent.*

ANTONIUS.

Who calls? I have been fast asleep. I dreamed.
Methought I held Salome in mine arms,
That, still a child, she smiled and prattled at
    me.
Then was she woman with a sad, sweet face,
Which rested on my bosom, and my beard
Bedecked with tears; then was she suddenly
Snatched from my folding arms by Hecate,
As was Proserpine by Pluto taken,
And vanished, vainly calling on my name.

KALIPHILUS.

'T was I who called. I would commune with
        thee.
I am a lone man: I would have a wife.

ANTONIUS.

Had I a dozen thou shouldst have them all.

KALIPHILUS.

If I should find thy daughter, promise me
That she shall wed me.

ANTONIUS.

                    She shall wed with thee?

KALIPHILUS.

Ay, so I said.

ANTONIUS.

She shall not.

KALIPHILUS.

Then farewell.

ANTONIUS.

Stay, stay. Who art thou?

KALIPHILUS.

I? a prince; thine equal.

ANTONIUS.

A man's my equal. I would know if thou
Hast manhood's majesty, its crown of truth,
Its sceptre honor, throne of probity,
A pedigree of honesty, a robe
Of justice, the device and crest of one
In his great dignity and full proportions,
Whose kingdom, thoroughly well ruled 's him-
        self.
My race is noblest; from the greatest gods
My blood, in streams ancestral, to my heart
Hath flowed. Yet hold I him in all my equal
In whom the gods have placed a noble soul.

KALIPHILUS.

Or ever the first stone of Troy was thought on
My ancestors were kings and talked with God.

ANTONIUS.

But what art thou thyself?   Thou askest not
My daughter for thine ancestors, but thee.

KALIPHILUS.

What have I done?   Did I not rescue thee,
A stranger?   Have I entertained thee well?

ANTONIUS.

'T is true.   I 'm not unmindful, nor ungrateful.

KALIPHILUS.

I seek thy daughter for her good and thine.

ANTONIUS.

And thine?

KALIPHILUS.

For mine, if it may be.

ANTONIUS.

Alas !
My daughter should have wed with Sextus ;
that

Is passed; he waiteth in the flowery groves
Of sweet Elysium for her.

KALIPHILUS.

Give her me.

ANTONIUS.

Thou lov'st her not. Engraft another stock
Upon thy heart, one thou hast known and loved.

KALIPHILUS.

To keep her were not to engraft; to lose
Were to break off a branch, which, to my
        heart,
Bears all the healthful influence of the skies.
I've lived to know when branches, torn away,
Leave wounds, comes weakness, blight, and rot;
        to know,
Alas, to feel, that when love once is dead
It hath no resurrection! If it seem
To move again 't is only its poor ghost
Appearing in the misty, dismal night.

ANTONIUS.

Thou canst not love her whom thou hast not
        seen.

KALIPHILUS.

But I have seen her.

ANTONIUS.

Thou ?

KALIPHILUS.

Yea, long ago,
And lately, by mine art.

ANTONIUS.

She lives ?

KALIPHILUS.

Ay, lives.

ANTONIUS.

She lives ? She lives !

KALIPHILUS.

Yea, and is well.

ANTONIUS.

She lives.
I thank ye, O immortal gods.   But where ?

KALIPHILUS.

When wouldst thou see her ?

ANTONIUS.

Now. Oh, bring me to her.

She 's mine — what, know'st thou not ? she is
    my child.

KALIPHILUS.

If thou wilt make the pledge I ask of thee —

ANTONIUS.

Nay, ask not that; but all my wealth —

KALIPHILUS.

                            What 's wealth ?

ANTONIUS.

All that my power at Rome can win for thee ;
Yea, mine own self to be thy servant.

KALIPHILUS.

                                  Thou !

ANTONIUS.

Ay, all I have, save her.

KALIPHILUS.

                          But I want her.

ANTONIUS.

At least, then, let me see her.

KALIPHILUS.
> Give the pledge.

ANTONIUS.

Nay, let me look on her afar.

KALIPHILUS.
> Thy pledge.

ANTONIUS.

Gods! but this passeth patience.

KALIPHILUS.
> Pledge the pledge.

ANTONIUS, *drawing.*

By Hercules! thou shalt.

KALIPHILUS.
> Ah! thou forgettest.

Put up thy sword, it cannot hurt me.

ANTONIUS, *thrusting at him.*

> So.

[*The sword is turned aside as by an invisible shield, and falls*
from his hand.

What art thou?

KALIPHILUS.

One who fain would be thy son.

ANTONIUS.

Oh, pardon me. Thou hast not been a father,
Thou hast not sought through life to find thy
   child.
I am an old man, and my sun is setting;
Along the shores of day the leaden Styx
Now dully glimmers; on its farther side
The shore of night lies silent; beetling crags
Of darkness imminent rise, and are lost
In blacker darkness hanging overhead.
Before I cross I would embrace my child,
Would hold her in my arms, all mine, until
The kindly boatman Charon comes for me.
Oh, bring me to her; woo her if thou wilt,
And as she will she shall decide thy suit.
Let me look on her face — she is my child;
Oh, let me feel that I again am linked
To what comes after me, — that one shall keep
My images among her household gods,
And be assured that I no more am childless.

KALIPHILUS.

Thou shalt not see her till thou pledge thine aid
To make her wive me. She shall —

ANTONIUS.

Threaten not.

KALIPHILUS.

So be it as thou choosest; I can wait
Thy sluggish promise : be it not too late.

A Wood.

ULLIN AND ORLA.

ULLIN.

SHE 's pure as dew.

ORLA.

And cold as snow.

ULLIN.

Nay, melts
As easily in pity's rays as that
In the sun's. She 's beautiful as evening fair,
A's constant as the day, benign as night.

ORLA.

Hast thou made known to her thy love?

ULLIN.

I have.

ORLA.

And now —

ULLIN.

My soul, once married to a hope,
Is widowed; and my dreams, like mists made
　　golden
By the new risen sun, then by it chased,
Have vanished.

ORLA.

Let them go, they were but mists.

ULLIN.

Ay, but they made this world so beautiful.
Now see I naught before me but a waste,
A dreary moor with wintry clouds and winds.

ORLA.

Nay, be a man, detest her for an ingrate —

ULLIN.

She owes me naught; and were she in my debt
For favors numberless as love would lavish
And think her creditor, accepting them,
Her gratitude should not lead love in chains.
And, priceless as her love, were it so brought,
I 'd set it free.

ORLA.

She 's weakly false or vain,

For thou art very fair and honorable ;
Thy love a glory for the proudest head
Which e'er in morning hues arose above
The gleaming slopes of a fair woman's shoulders.

ULLIN.

I think her soul hath widowed been as mine
Is now. She spoke so gently, and her voice
Was like the mourning south wind when it comes
And leads with either hand a weeping cloud.
Upon each cheek, and weighing down each lid,
A crowd of tears protested solemnly
That she was neither weak, nor false, nor vain.

ORLA.

What! was she moved?

ULLIN.

      Ay, as a placid lake
When a spring torrent takes her in his arms.
Her soft hands trembled as the white rose when
The north wind seizes it ; her bosom moved
As lilies, when in troubled waves a storm
Upheaves the peaceful waters where they rest.

ORLA.

So said thee nay?

ULLIN.

E'en thus.

ORLA.

And meant it ?

ULLIN.

Ay.

ORLA.

What wouldst thou now ?

ULLIN.

I 'd · save her.

ORLA.

Save ? From what ?

ULLIN.

From death. No Roman captive can be found
To be a victim for the sacrifice,
When we shall hold to-night the annual feast
And celebrate with rites the Roman wreck,
Propitiate the gods to curse our foes
And seek their aid against the world's great king.
A plot to slay her groweth now apace,
To immolate her for the sacrifice.
The wicked Ranmor shall Kaliphilus

Assail with force persuasive that he grant
Salome to his vengeance and bad zeal.

ORLA.

A solemn convocation shall be held,
Already by swift messengers proclaimed;
And if Kaliphilus should feebly yield,
The druid chief, the white-haired Alpindargo,
Shall then uproot the plot and save his pet.
He 'll not consent.

ULLIN.

He vainly may withstand,
His strength and policy be overthrown
In the debate, by union of her foes,
The druid college, jealous of her faith.

ORLA.

Then plannest thou in vain : thou canst not save
her.

ULLIN.

I must.

ORLA.

But how?

ULLIN.

I 'll seek Kaliphilus
The great magician.

5

ORLA.

Well.

ULLIN.

And so beseech
That he cannot deny my prayer, but shall
Refuse to render her, or point the way
For me to rescue her.

ORLA.

How can he do it?

ULLIN.

By his deep art.

ORLA.

And will he?

ULLIN.

Ay, he must.

ORLA.

Must, must, how sayest thou must?

ULLIN.

I love her, man,
And love says must: love is omnipotent.

ORLA.

Then love may rescue her.

ULLIN.

It shall, by means.
Wilt come with me ? I seek him now ; he 'll
      help.
He hath befriended her.

OBLA.

See, here he comes !

Enter KALIPHILUS.

ULLIN.

I sought thee.

KALIPHILUS.

Then well met. Come to my tent.

ULLIN.

Nay, if it please thee, we will here commune.
Salome is in danger; o'er her head
The death cloud pauses; mists are gathering
      now
To lift her ghost; the airy halls are bright
For her approach ; the gods are leaning forth
Expecting her ; and spirits —

KALIPHILUS.

Talk plain sense.
Salome is in danger ? What ? From whom ?

ULLIN.

She shall be sacrificed this night to Hesus
Unless thou save her.

KALIPHILUS.

   Ha! he loves her; then
She him. It is for him she spurns me. So,
A dangerous rival; loyal, generous —

ULLIN.

O save her; thou canst do it; thy power is
  great.
Thy mighty arts can find a rescue for her.

KALIPHILUS.

My mighty arts shall move him from my path,—
Young, and so brave,—he 's fool enough to do it.

ULLIN.

Dost thou not hear me?

ORLA.

   Look! his gaze is fixed
Upon the distant air; and from their caves
His eyes are rushing; deep convulsions shake
His solid frame: stand back! disturb him not.

ULLIN.

The spell is on him, — he shall see the way
For her deliverance.

ORLA.

How dread must be
The vision. Stand we further back; the gods
Are talking with him.

ULLIN.

Hist! it passes! Hist!

KALIPHILUS.

Approach, ye bards, approach.

ULLIN.

What hast thou seen?

KALIPHILUS.

I may not tell thee, but the gods have spoken
In dreadful form and words.

ULLIN.

What is their will?

KALIPHILUS.

She must be sacrificed; else shall the Romans

Return, slay, devastate, and living, burn
Bards, druids, all upon your altar pyres,
A sacrifice unto the gods of Rome.
The gods of Briton will not be despised;
Gods in Jow's misty halls shall never yield
To those of high Olympus. She must die.

ULLIN.

Is there no way to save her?

KALIPHILUS.

None, but one.

ULLIN.

And that —

KALIPHILUS.

Knowest thou if she be loved?

ULLIN.

She is.

KALIPHILUS.

By one who loves her more than every love?

ULLIN.

Yea, truly.

KALIPHILUS.

More than lovers ever loved her?

ULLIN.

I 'll swear it.

KALIPHILUS.

More than life?

ULLIN.

Than life, or hope,
Or fame.

KALIPHILUS.

So well that, for her sake, he 'd live
For, but without her?

ULLIN.

Ay.

KALIPHILUS.

Or for her die?

ULLIN.

Yea, fifty deaths to save her from one pain.
A thousand lovers, each bestowing all,
Could not make up the sum of love he owns
For her.

KALIPHILUS.

What! loveth he so well?   Beware
Thou pledge him not too rashly lest he fail.
Could he be found, and would he give himself
A victim to propitiate the gods —

ULLIN.

Could he so save her?

KALIPHILUS.

So the gods declare.

ULLIN.

The gods be thanked.   I here declare myself
The victim.

KALIPHILUS.

Thou?

ULLIN.

I love her.

KALIPHILUS.

Then Amen.

ORLA.

What! art thou mad?   Thou canst not, — shalt
not do it.

No priest shall serve thee for so fell a deed.
Thy father Alpindargo leads the rites.

ULLIN.

He may not do it. When he shall know that she
Is to be offered he 'll withdraw himself,
And, prostrate, weeping in his cave alone,
Mourn for her. By the storm of grief his age
Be shaken ; and perchance, his feeble limbs,
Grief-spent, refuse to bring him to the feast.
Nay, nay, I 'll find a way to overcome
All that withstands, and safely to forestall
The slow and formal priest. Thou 'lt have a
    care,
Lest in a moment's fury she be found
And slain by the impatient crowd, that she
Be placed in some safe covert, where no rage
Can find her. Wilt thou promise me ?

KALIPHILUS.

I will.

ULLIN.

The great gods bless thee. Fare thee well.

KALIPHILUS.

Farewell.

[*Exeunt* ULLIN *and* ORLA.

Ha, ha, ha, ha! Well done, Kaliphilus!
Well acted prophet! Well achieved, O knave!
Yet 't is not he she loves, — not he, poor fool.
He loves too much to be beloved in turn,
Too loyal, frank to keep a woman's love.
He doth not make her anxious, torture her,
And seem forever slipping from her grasp:
So would she tighten it, and all her strength,
Thoughts, tenderness, desires of her soul
Devote to holding him still fast to her;
And bind about him, thus to hold him chained,
The ever-strengthening tendrils of her love;
So bind herself to him ever more firmly.
But she may love him when she hears he's
        dead,
And so escaped from her capricious will,
If she know why he died. She must not know
        it.
Or better 't were he die not: he shall live.
She loves him not; ay, let the youth then live
And suffer. Why should I hold to his lips
Death's chalice sweet, which to my lips in vain
I lift, but cannot drain? Yea he shall live.
I will with subtle Ranmor straight confer.
The game goes on: while they enjoy the pain
Of being moved, I move them for my gain.

SEXTUS.

I SHOULD be near the hill which from the shore
I saw, or this is an enchanted isle.
Could I but reach its summit unobserved —
Or have I lost my course ? — from there I 'd
    spy
The sun's track and the secrets of this land,
And with impatient vision read the seas,
And learn if aught but me escaped the wreck.
I saw Antonius with his ship engulfed ;
But yet, perchance, some others of the fleet
Outfought the storm, and safely won a haven.
Still prudence guide, and caution be my guard.
Oh for a hundred trusty men well armed, —
Ay fifty, twenty, even ten of mine, —
I 'd skulk no more about this gloomy wood,
Nor longer play the fox, but lionlike
Spring on my foes at once. Ye gods ! it irks
    me,
And frets my patience that I here must lurk.
' T were strange indeed if none of mine like me
Outran the waves and safely came ashore,

Or there were thrown.   If I alone so lived,
As I shall learn if 1 can reach the hill,
I 'll sell my life as dearly as I can
To the first force of Britons who dare buy it,
And join my friends in Hades.

Enter KALIPHILUS.

KALIPHILUS.

Eh! a Roman?

SEXTUS.

But if some of my fellows were preserved,
With prudence still we may retrieve our loss
And overmount disaster.

KALIPHILUS.

Ah, a chief!
A Roman general! now he is mine!
The prowling fiends are leagued to aid me.
Good!
I will encounter him.

SEXTUS.

As well be hemmed
By midnight's barriers as this foliage.

KALIPHILUS.

Nay, 'sir, methinks the foliage is better.

SEXTUS, *drawing and advancing on him.*

Ha!

KALIPHILUS.

Be not rash; thou art choleric — or timid,
To let an interruption anger thee.
I am alone, and, as thou seest, unarmed.

SEXTUS.

How callest thou thyself?

KALIPHILUS.

A traveler.

SEXTUS.

And so are all of us. What is thy name?

KALIPHILUS.

One that I would forget, and none should learn.

SEXTUS.

Thou art skillful at thy fence. But what art
thou?

KALIPHILUS.

Ask Him who made me.

SEXTUS.

Pray, what was his trade?

KALIPHILUS.

An image-maker.

SEXTUS.

Say a poet, rather.
He made strange images.

KALIPHILUS.

'T is true, He did,
To mar, defile, degrade, and then to burn.
To see how He could mix up God and devil
To make a thing that's neither; they are men
In whom the mixture's equal; all the rest
Are creatures which should be without a name.
When both are equal contest shall endure,
And strife's the soul of man. From thence
      shoot forth
Great manhood crystallized in daring act
Or glowing thought, an offspring that's immortal;
As precious things are to the surface thrown
Of the deep working earth by conflict fierce
Of elements within.

SEXTUS.

Hast been long here?

KALIPHILUS.

Much longer than I would, yet not so long.

SEXTUS.

What mak'st thou?

KALIPHILUS.

Answer questions, sometimes ask them.

SEXTUS.

Thine answers are but foils; they serve to parry,
Thou dost not with them pierce the understand-
ing.
What isle is this? What sea? What yonder
land?

KALIPHILUS.

The isle of Mona: British sea and land.

SEXTUS.

What are these Britons?

KALIPHILUS.

They 're a servile race,
Although they boast they 're not; they ape their
great ones;
But boasting is their chief accomplishment.
A people strong in the hips and good to fight
With any people weaker than themselves
To whom they 're full of most offensive pride.
But to a people, who, they think is strong,
They 're very courteous, and even will

Walk backward, so that thou wouldst almost
        swear
They had some culture of civility.
They seem to think themselves God's constables
For all the world; that there can be no fight
But they are in to break a head or two
Upon the weaker party. But they wait
Until they think they know which side shall win,
And then they help it, so that they may say
They 've kept the peace of the world. For
        them the world
Is, chiefly, their own island; all the rest
Is appanages which should be protected.

                    SEXTUS.

I marvel that thou dwell'st in safety here,
For, though 't is plain thou art no Roman, yet
Barbarians, such as these, should think thee so.

                  KALIPHILUS.

One who cannot be harmed is always safe.
Now tell me whence art thou ?

                    SEXTUS.

                        Last from the sea.

                  KALIPHILUS.

I 'll call thee Triton.

SEXTUS.

Nay, a Roman soldier,
Whose ship was broken near the towering cliffs
Within the caverns of whose arched foundations
The waves have caged the thunders, and yet
  guard
Them roaring there.

KALIPHILUS.

I saw thy ship astride
A rearing billow keeping well its place,
Like skilful rider, for one moment; then
I saw it flung into the dark abyss
And trampled on, as, by a wild horse thrown,
I 've seen a stripling die.

SEXTUS.

An hour thence
I was alone upon the throbbing shore.

KALIPHILUS.

No one could say which of them loudest shrieked,
The sea or sky.

SEXTUS.

Yea, they did split their throats
With bellowing; and through the mists I saw
The roaring Neptune with his helmet on,

6

Which, with its waving, snow-white plumage
    seemed
A mountain top, o'er which great waters break
In glittering foam; his towering helm alone
Above the surface reared, with his huge arms
He pushed the howling billows from beneath,
And smote resounding caverns with his feet
As on he strode and shook the central earth.

KALIPHILUS.

This island on its firm foundation quaked
As it had felt a blow which staggered it.

SEXTUS.

Perchance he put his trident underneath
With purpose to uplift and cast it at
The heavens also.

KALIPHILUS.

          All is still again.

SEXTUS.

But better I like tumult of such battle
Than such a stillness after such defeat.
Then was there hope — now none.

KALIPHILUS.

          What is thy name?

SEXTUS.

One I am not ashamed of — Sextus.

KALIPHILUS.

Ah !
She should have wed with Sextus, said her
    father.
A double prize ! Indeed thou sayest well
A spotless name ; thou hast made fame thy hand-
    maid :
Obsequious she wears thy colors.

SEXTUS.

Hold —

KALIPHILUS.

Rumor precedes and valor follows thee.
Forgive me that I may have been too bold,
And let me make what poor amends I may.
Rest here, while, from my poor abode near by,
I bring thee some refreshment.

SEXTUS.

That were kind.
I 'd gladly break my fast, somewhat too long
Already.

KALIPHILUS.

In a place of safety then
I will bestow thee, for the isle is full

Of hostile Britons; while my couriers,
Of vision keen, swift as the wing-heeled god,
In ambient course shall quickly bring me word
If any of thy comrades have survived,
And how to join thee to them.

SEXTUS.

Thanks, kind sir;
If thou do this thou shalt no more deny
Thy name. I'll make it so the sun at noon
As easily were hidden.

KALIPHILUS.

Rest you, sir.
[*Exit* KALIPHILUS.

SEXTUS.

Now if he should betray me — if he should —
Sometimes there's safety in an if. I'll wait, —
The more that Destiny hath left no choice
For Prudence here. — A curious animal!
He hath a traitor's face, spite of his beauty;
His voice repels me, though so sweetly sad.
His eyes are those of an old man; they're deep,
Ay, deep enough to mirror all a future.
And in them burns no fitful flame of youth,
But unveiled fire of full experience,
Which shines therein, as in a lake's deep centre
The troubled image of the mid-day sun.

Upon their shores are haunts of disappointments ;
Of sorrows such as come at middle life,
And signs of hopeless grief, which only live
In age's wintry season ; on his brow,
In darkening shades, are gathering evening
    clouds,
But still his head bears spring-like foliage.
No frosts have fallen on his growing beard ;
In his complexion all the bloom of youth
Vies with the overshadowing hues of health ;
Yet on his face are channels made alone
By evening's deeply flowing tide of thought.
And o'er his mouth an image dark of woe
Enshrinèd sits and never leaves its place.
While sneers, the ghostly semblances of smiles,
Are haunting the dark portals of his speech.
What may he be ? I cannot him define.
The waves of passion rolling on his face
Have left upon that shore the tracks of storms,
Of tides o'ermounting every barrier.
But, so he bring me food and treat me well,
I 'll call him Jove's own son, if so he will.

Before a Cave hollowed among overhanging Rocks in the Bank of a deep Glen.

TORSA AND THREE PIRATES.

TORSA.

OUR master hath no plot to-day; we 're idle.

FIRST PIRATE.

Fear not, we shall have work enough.

SECOND PIRATE.

Ay, ay,
If it were but to keep us from our ease.

THIRD PIRATE.

He never rests.

TORSA.

If we should plot for him —

THIRD PIRATE.

'T would cost us dear. I have not yet forgot
The torments he put on us when we tried
To circumvent him.

TORSA.

I 'd endure again
Tenfold such tortures, could we get possession
Of that fair captive which he took from us.

FIRST PIRATE.

Ere we could profit by her —

TORSA.

Sure he thinks
We serve him here and bear his gibes and blows
Because we fear him; but we bide our time.
Eh ?

ALL THREE.

Yea, we bide our time.

TORSA.

We 'll catch him yet
Asleep ; then for revenge — eh, fellows ?

ALL THREE.

Ay,
Revenge.

TORSA.

And booty.

ALL THREE.

Ay, and booty.

TORSA.

And —

Is that all, boys ?

ALL THREE.

And love — his sweet Salome.
Ha, ha !

TORSA.

Hush ! there he comes.

SECOND PIRATE.

Where ?

TORSA.

On the bank.

Enter KALIPHILUS.

KALIPHILUS.

Up louts, and take your arms.

ALL FOUR.

We have them.

KALIPHILUS.

Quick,
Come here.   Thou, Torsa, take this food ; nay,
      leave
Thine arms with me ; the rest of ye go armed.
Upon the hill-side, near the oak, whose boughs
Are wrinkles on the aged brow of heaven,

Ye 'll find a Roman : haste, proceed with care,
Take him alive ; and, that ye may do so,
And keep your own lives, come upon him slyly.
While Torsa brings, unarmed, this food to him,
And entertains him with kind messages
From me, the rest of ye shall come about,
Unseen by him ; approach him from behind,
Spring on and bind him. He is armed, and
    brave —
See that ye wound him not ; and bring him
    thence
Into your den, and keep him safely there.
If he escape, or if ye do him harm,
Ye know how I can punish.

ALL FOUR.

Fear us not.

A Hill-side.

THONA.

LET 's sit upon the moss, the royal bed
On which the fairy king and queen repose.

SALOME.

Here first I saw thee.

THONA.

            I remember well.
Kaliphilus had brought thee to my father,
Who, as chief Druid, could decree thy fate.

SALOME.

He, by Kaliphilus persuaded, brought
Me here to thee.

THONA.

            To be my dear companion.
But little thought he that I should become
A Christian, and abjure the old religion.
I have not dared to tell him what I am,
For he would cause us to be sacrificed

Unto his gods, — he's so obedient
To his dark faith, and stern in druid zeal.

SALOME.

His zeal is honest, but is led astray :
So honesty, too oft, takes the wrong way.

THONA.

Salome, lovest thou Kaliphilus ?

SALOME.

Why askest thou ?

THONA.

To make thee tell. For me,
I like him not. I never am at ease
When he is near. So seems to shrink my soul
And tremble in his presence, as I 've seen
Our dove, when hawks approach, shake in its
cote.

SALOME.

Thou art dove-like timid, mine own gentle dove.

THONA.

I 've heard my father talk of this strange be-
ing,
And he believes him to be more than man, —
If not a god, yet of immortal race.
Hast thou been happy with me here ?

SALOME.

Thou knowest.

THONA.

Nay, frankly speak.

SALOME.

At first I was not; but
When I perceived how gentle and how good
Thou art, I was content; then loved thee; then
Would not part from thee.

THONA.

Thou art dear to me.
But would'st thou not revisit the loved place
In which thine infancy was passed?

SALOME.

If I
With thee might do so; but without thee, nay.

THONA.

In yonder beauteous valley, half concealed
By that low mountain lying in the shade
Of bright-winged clouds, a druid hamlet hides.
There was I born. About me happy brooks
All day were wandering, chanting all the night,
And virgin vines hung on the sturdy arms
Of youthful trees, and, whispering, swayed with
        them

A gentle dance to music of the breeze.
And sweet shrubs in the bosom of the brooks
Placed flowers slyly; or withdrew themselves
To central groves their beauties to unfold,
And on a veilèd altar offer up
The odorous incense from their censer cups.
'T is all before me now — so beautiful!
Shall heaven be like this, but more beautiful?

SALOME.

The Master hath not told us what, nor where,
How founded, of what builded heaven is.
'T is where the glorious majesty of God
Pervades, its awful beauty may be seen,
And all His lovely attributes be felt,
And all His great perfections by us known,
Not as by gods, but as by men perfected.
And so our adoration, which belongs
Alone to spirits finite, be complete, —
A springing, endless joy.

THONA.

But where is heaven?
Is it above the sky?

SALOME.

For me, I think
That heaven is in us, that we are heaven

Unto ourselves, when we are so perfected
That we perceive unclouded, and so feel,
In perfect ecstasy and strength, all beauty,
Of which the chiefest is of Holiness
The beauty; whose harmonious perfections
Throb on our souls as breezes on a harp.
And all these sinful chords so out of tune,
Which jar discordant passions in us now,
Shall then, attuned, yield sweetest harmony.
It hath been called for us a state of rest,
Because our weakness is so great that we
Are always weary; but I think that there
We shall be so perfected we can feel
No weariness, or need no rest, and thus
The rest of heaven is absence of fatigue.
In this imperfect state our joys all spring
From action, just as music only comes
From chords in motion; yet it wearies us.
But there, breathed on by beauty, we shall
        thrill
Forever with harmonious joys, which yet
Grow stronger, richer, more harmonious,
As viols played on grow forever sweeter.
And this perfected action in perfection,
Forever acting, never wearying,
And causing joy complete in ecstasy,
Shall but express our still increasing love.
Wilt thou not sing for me?

THONA.

What shall I sing?

SALOME.

I pray thee sing the hymn which last I taught
thee.

THONA *sings.*

Weary, with sin opprest,
Not, Lord, complaining,
Oh, bring me to the rest
For Thine remaining.

Take, take me by the hand,
The seas roll o'er me,
And lead me to the land
I see before me.

My days of trial told,
My sinning ended,
My lambs all in the fold
By Thee defended,

Cleansed, with Thy seal imprest,
By love constraining,
Lift, lift me to Thy breast,
Thou All-sustaining.

SALOME.

I thank thee, — sweet the prayer on music
    borne
'T is like burnt-offerings which mount on in-
    cense.

THONA.

Salome, wouldst thou truly like to die?

SALOME.

To die, for life means death, and death means
    life, —
That endless bliss.

THONA.

        But I so love this life.
I am as in a Paradise like Eden.
The sweetest flowers about my feet, above
To reach me bending, stooping to my hand
On either side, and playful joining arms
Before to stop my way, which stretches on
Through an ascending vale whose lateral bounds
Are gentle hills reclining, holding groves
Like nosegays in their bosoms; on whose brows
The laurel and the palm branch wave; whose
    robes
Are verdant velvets wove on noiseless looms
In shady grottos underneath the earth,
By Spring's fair virgin daughters; broidered o'er
With violets, forget-me-nots, and roses,

From dew - drops wrought by Morning's busy
    sprites.
Midway the vale, instead of flowers, fruits
Of every golden hue, purple and white
And roseate, scarlet, crimson, fading green,
As immature comes to maturity,
Invite me on to life's delicious feast :
And thence the valley winds through thickening
    shade
Of forests growing tall and dense and dark,
To hills that tower in a sunset light,
Like ranges of midsummer clouds made bright
By Evening walking on them, and her robes
Long trailing far adown their craggy sides.

SALOME.

Ah, such was mine; O joyful youth, alas !

THONA.

The air is full of music which the ear
Can hear not, but the soul still feels; and light
That fills the heart with gladness, all made up
Of evening twilight, moonlight, light of dawn
Together blending, as in music blend
Sweet tones accordant, when they so unite
That none can tell whose is the voice that soars
In highest strains, nor whose the deepest moves.
The streamlets in the lakes unite as souls

7

In heaven; which is reflected from them all
As from the face of an unbroken mirror.
And all who dwell here love me; all I meet
Caress. Such seems this life to me.

SALOME.

Alas!

Such unto me was once life's vista; now
It stretches through a valley dark and drear,
Whose flowers, killed in their fresh bloom, hang
      pale
And odorless; no fruits are there to ripen.
Its bounds are fire-blackened crags; its streams
Cold, flinty, lava motionless; its lakes
The Dead Sea's bitterness; its only groves
The silent ghosts of trees casting no shadow;
Its softest paths the broken pointed rocks,
Which wind a tortuous, long, and drear extent.
But where it terminates a cross I see, —
A hill, like Calvary; beyond the cross
A gate, like crystal, made of light concrete,
Which shines upon my way — so bright the sun
Would pale before it, and so soft the moon
Shoots in comparison bright rays of steel.
And from the cross I hear a voice say, *Come!*
Which fills my soul more than all harmonies
With longing, gladness, joy unspeakable.
Thy earthly life is bright; no blight on thee

Hath fallen ; in the very bud my life
Was blasted.

THONA.

Yet thou art happy.

SALOME.

Yea, I am.
He so hath loved me.

THONA.

Oh that I, too, were
So gentle, lovely, loving as thou art!

SALOME.

I 'll go and find Bernice : she 's unhappy.

THONA.

What aileth her ?

SALOME.

Ah, that I know not. Come.

THONA.

Nay, go alone ; 't were better thus. I 'll stay.
[*Exit* SALOME.

They say that lovers only are unhappy,
And that it is their greatest happiness.
But when I love — ah me ! whom shall I love ?
[*Sings.*

There was a gentle maiden,
   As fair as fair could be ;
This fair and gentle maiden
   Sat by the sounding sea.

This fair and gentle maiden
   Cried, *Come, love, come to me;*
And, from the sea foam-laden,
   A voice replied, — *To thee,*

To thee, O gentle maiden,
   I come with joy and glee;
O fair and gentle maiden,
   Open thine arms to me.

Then from the waters foaming,
   As brave as brave could be,
Aweary with his roaming
   Through trackless wastes of sea,

A fair sea-god, appearing,
   As gentle mists appear,
Came to the maiden fearing
   A lover, when so near.

He put his arms about her,
   He whispered in her ear —
He could not live without her,
   And wept a briny tear.

His voice was like the sighing
  Of breezes in the spring,
When, in the sunlight dying,
  They faint upon the wing.

He pressed the maiden to him,
  He felt her heart beat fast;
Its beating seemed to woo him, —
  Thou art mine, thou art mine at last,

He said, and still more tightly
  The gentle maiden pressed;
She sighed, and then more lightly
  The heart beat in her breast.

She sighed, and then she shivered:
  More tightly her he pressed;
Tears on her eyelids quivered,
  Still her the god caressed.

The cold came slowly creeping
  Up, up into her heart;
She cried, with bitter weeping,
  O lover mine, depart.

Thine arms of snow enclose me,
  All icy is thy breast,
Thy wintry breath hath froze me, —
  Alas, for love confest!

He still more closely to him
 The gentle maiden pressed;
Her weeping seemed to woo him;
 More fondly he caressed.

But ah! O gentle maiden,
 Fixed now thine eye appears,
Thine eyelids heavy laden
 With weight of frozen tears;

Ceased has thy heart's wild beating;
 Thy heaving bosom rests;
And, through thy lips, not meeting,
 Appear thy teeth's white crests.

The sea-god takes her lightly,
 And bears her to the sea;
And there she shineth brightly,
 As bright as bright can be.

Yet there she never smileth,
 But, cold as cold can be,
No warmth her heart beguileth
 In the far, northern sea.

For there she now is roaming,
 The sea-god by her side,
Through trackless waters foaming
 His frozen, icy bride.

And, when the tall ships see her —
　An Iceberg! loud they cry ;
And none attempt to free her,
　But, frightened, pass her by.

Now, look, each gentle maiden
　Who sittest by the sea,
Some god with kisses laden
　Come not a-wooing thee.

Ah me ! Had I a lover he should not
Freeze me; I 'd melt him with a genial
　.　　warmth,
Nor ever wish to free me from his arms,
Nor ever think his path a trackless waste.
Where'er he went should be my flowery mead ;
He all things for me: I should nothing need.

A Grove.

BERNICE.

BERNICE.

Ah! she shall lie
  Where I have lain,
And sigh and weep
  With love's sweet pain,

In those dear arms
  So gently strong,
Near that dear heart,
  So sad and wrong.

Shall feel his breath,
  Shall have his kiss,
Shall have, ah me!
  All my lost bliss.

Too hard to bear!
  Oh I would die,
Yield love, my life,
  In one dear sigh.

And yet he will not love her; will love me,
If I can win her; but his shall she be.
And she will love him — ay, but me he 'll love.
She be the cuckoo, I his mated dove.
Then must I win her. Jealousy, be still,
And let love be as foolish as love will.

Enter SALOME.

SALOME.

Bernice, what! my friend, in tears?

BERNICE.

Alas!

SALOME.

Unhappiness hath taken the citadel
Of thine oppressèd heart, and spread abroad
Its banners o'er the fair field of thy face;
And in thine eyes, its watch-towers, hath it
placed
A glittering garrison of ready tears;
And from thy parted lips, its archèd portal,
Sends sounding signs, its heralds, to proclaim
Thee subjugated. Let us dispossess
This most oppressive tyrant; reinstate
The rightful ruler, Cheerfulness, and make
Smiles, its bright ensigns, beam from every part
Of this fair territory. Nay, look up,
And weep no more. What aileth thee, my
friend?

BERNICE.

Alas! I cannot tell thee.

SALOME.

                              ·Sit by me,
And let me know thy grief.

BERNICE.

                              Would that I could.
My heart is crushed with woe.

SALOME.

                              Weep silently
Upon my breast, and feel my sympathy.
Impart, or keep thy sorrow, as thou wilt,
But tell me how to help thee.

BERNICE.

                              Let me weep,
And feel thine arms about me — so — alas!

SALOME.

Such showers fertilize the heart, and bring
Its richest plants to blossom; so the soul
Is clad in verdure, else an arid waste.

BERNICE.

Salome, canst thou love Kaliphilus?

SALOME.

I love Kaliphilus? How mean'st thou love?

BERNICE.

Nay, answer me. I know he loveth thee.

SALOME.

How knowest thou?

BERNICE.

Since last he came from thee
I know naught of him, save his outward form.
His clouded face to me is like the dull,
Unchanging, sunless days, which solemnly
Stand round dead nature, and receive the winter
Soft coming to enshroud and bury her.
He stands or wanders idly; seems like one
In whom the throne of Reason is usurped,
And all its fair light-bearing train expelled
By shadow-leading and black-robed Despair.

SALOME.

What wrought this in him?

BERNICE.

What but love for thee
Uncheered by hope! He rests his darkened
brow,

Which grows more dark, not as with gathering
    storms,
But slow descending Night, upon his hands;
Anon he utters broken parts of phrases,
Which seem like wrecks of thought thrown on
    the shore
Of sense by the subsiding storm.

SALOME.

What words?

BERNICE.

Borne by his sighs I gather such as these:
Lost! lost! she might have saved me, none but
    she:
To live, and live, and live, but not with her
Nor for her. She to scorn a soul condemned
For her sweet sake! Why, such a love as mine
Should make a devil worthy. Long-drawn
    groans,
Which scarcely can be heard, so deep they come,
Attest the inward fires which shake his frame.
His gaze sees neither earth, nor sea, nor air.
'T is turned upon that blighted, inward world,
Which, back reflected from his heavy eyes,
Shows its dull image in the duller orbs.

SALOME.

That is not love; it hath not that complexion.
It is a fire that permeates the soul,

Which kindles in the eye, glows on the cheek,
Beams on the brow, as on the eastern sky
The rising sun ; unbinds the fettered currents,
And, spring-like, sends them bounding to the
    heart,
Which thrills with their commotion ; 't is some
    sorrow
That overwhelms his soul ; think not 't is love.

BERNICE.

Oh, tell me so again — I mean not that.
Nay, nay, he loves thee well : know'st thou a
    grief
More terrible than that whence no tears come,
Which bends the heart down to the earth before
The tomb of buried friendship, or the shrine
Of vanished love ?

SALOME.

Nay. Is there aught more woful ?

BERNICE.

The woe of love itself unfed by hope,
Shut from the heavenly air of promises,
And lighted by no star of sympathy, —
For perfect love is sympathy's perfection.
Such love is woe — woe that undoes itself
But to be greater. When poor love is starved,

And shut from this same wholesome air of
    heaven,
It loses health, is changed, and turns to mad-
    ness.

SALOME.

All love is gentle madness, is it not?

BERNICE.

Most gentle and most sweet, when happy, like
The intoxication which, the Grecians say,
Their gods enjoy. Yet 't is not madness; no,
But best estate of health.

SALOME.

                How knowest thou
Its qualities? Hast thou, too, loved?

BERNICE.

                      Alas !—
But I came not to speak to thee of mine,
Of his love rather. That he loves thee well
I think thou knowest; that thou hast been hard
With him, his constant sighs declare. Why so?
Is he not worthy? Is he not a prince?
Doth not his tongue make music? and his eyes—
Are they not loadstones to a woman's soul?
Are not his movements full of softest grace,
So that they seem to weave a magic spell
About the heart?

SALOME.

Of what avail were it?
I could not wed.

BERNICE.

What! must this earth so rich
Be barren? This fair wilderness, so fit
A garden, all become a withered waste?
Why, look thou, shall this virgin bust, these limbs,
Which glow with fullest blossoms of the spring,
Where all the softest forms of beauty meet,
Bear their warm bloom in vain?

SALOME.

Fie! foolish girl.

BERNICE.

Nay, listen to me. Wilt thou not permit
The other half of thy perfected being
To gather these rare fruits?

SALOME.

Hush, hush! Bernice.

BERNICE.

I say thou art but half of one complete;
Nor I: none of us are.

SALOME.

Yet we may be

Contented, when the yearning spirit finds
Communion, that is happiness, with Heaven.

BERNICE.

But that compounded nature, half of soul,
Half sense, which spirit and material part
Holds knit as true love holds the truly wedded,
So that, one touched, both feel — one hurt, both
      weep;
That sea of deep emotions in our breasts,
Wherein the heavens are brokenly reflected,
While underneath dark Hades lies concealed
Perchance to whelm these heavens in a storm,
By its upheaving; this compounded part
Can ne'er be satisfied save with its kind,
Longs for communion with that which for it
Is best of earth, yet worse than worst in heaven;
Divine in form, and clothed upon, alas!
Too much, by that idolater, the heart,
With the divine perfections; longs to feel
Its arms encircle of itself that half
So strangely lost in some anterior life, —

SALOME.

And oft, ah me! so vainly sought in this!
I loved: my love is lost; I cannot find him.

BERNICE.

Then take another.

SALOME.

Nay, I could not do it.

BERNICE.

Thy love is dead?

SALOME.

Alas! I fear he is.
He would not so keep silence if he lived.
So many years I've waited for a word
Responsive to the messages I sent.
Such pleadings had provoked a stone to tears
Of pardon. Yet he comes not, sends no sign.
But, till I surely know him dead, I'll wed
No other.

BERNICE.

And then —

SALOME.

Ah, then! I have not thought
Of that.

BERNICE.

But, could'st thou love Kaliphilus?

SALOME.

He hath been very kind.

BERNICE.

Then thou dost love him.

SALOME.

I said not so.

BERNICE.

Thou dost, thou dost. O me!

SALOME.

What! tears again! — more tears!

BERNICE.

Alas, alas!

SALOME.

How have I grieved thee?

BERNICE.

I must tell thee all,
Or break my heart.

SALOME.

Be comforted.

BERNICE.

Ah, me!
No bosom opens its embossèd gates
To give my sorrows cheer; no friendliness
Comes ,forth to meet, and bid them to repose;
No minstrelsy of gentle words expels
Their heaviness, for I am friendless here.

SALOME.

Come to my bosom ; hear my gentle words,
And rest, for I would be thy friend.

BERNICE.

Alas !
Thou know'st me not.

SALOME.

I know thou art unhappy.

BERNICE.

Oh, do not spurn me if I tell thee all,
For I must tell thee, and so find relief,
And be as honest as I now can be.
Thy kindness melts my armor of deceit
And shows me to thee naked, as I am.
I love Kaliphilus.

SALOME.

I know thou dost,
As should a sister.

BERNICE.

I am not his sister.

SALOME.

Art not his sister ?

BERNICE.

Oh ! I 'm not, I 'm not.

SALOME.

But art thou then his daughter?

BERNICE.

No — oh no.

SALOME.

Nor niece, nor cousin? Wife thou canst not be.

BERNICE.

Alas! I 'm neither.

SALOME.

But what art thou then?

BERNICE.

O spare me.   Something which thou canst not
name.

SALOME.

My poor, poor child.

BERNICE.

And thou abhorr'st me not?

SALOME.

I pity thee.

BERNICE.

The God in heaven bless thee —
So wretched am I.

SALOME.

Yea, I know, I know.
But if thou lov'st why would'st thou that I
wed him?

BERNICE.

To purchase thus again what I have lost.
He promised me that, were he wed to thee,
He would not love thee, — would love only me.
And so I 've urged thee, as I 'd plead for life,
No, not to love him, but to be his wife.
Then can I bear it better. Love him not;
Who love are aye unhappy; take the lot
Of wives unloving.

SALOME.

So hath promised thee —
And thou would'st trust him still?

BERNICE.

'T is my soul's habit:
I have so loved, and trusted him, and lived
But in a world of which he was the god,
As if transformed or new created by him,
I wait the re-arising of his love
As for the sun in storms, or day in night.
His promises have been my breath of life,
And faith in him was, as it were, my soul.
To be with him was the eternity

Of joy for which I looked, expected, prayed, —
The object and fruition of my life.
And all his sorrows but increased my love.

SALOME.

And he had wooed thee ?

BERNICE.

Wooed me as the Sun
Woos the warm Earth in spring, and draws
    from her
Confessions loath, sweet flowers half unfolding.

SALOME.

And having won he loved thee — loves thee
    still ?

BERNICE.

He loves me not; and I must see thee take
The place with honor which I held with shame.
But were I pure again, like thee, I'd bear
The pangs of unrequited love, the thorns
Of lacerating jealousy, and think
Them heavenly joys; for now I suffer tortures
Of shame, remorse, and hopelessness, like those
Of hell.

SALOME.

Despair not; thou may'st find relief.

BERNICE.

Nay, I can never be but what I am,
And being what I am must suffer still
These tortures.

SALOME.

Yea, thou canst again be blessed,
When thy strength faileth thee, in One whose
strength
Sufficeth. He is ever nigh to help.
Come in with me.

BERNICE.

Thou wilt not love him then?

Before a Hut in a scathed Grove of Pines.

THONA.

THONA.

My father said that I might find him here;
I wish he would not see the man. All fear
This place; and 't is no wonder, for the trees,
All blasted, stand like watchful ghosts about
The spot. They say that yonder hut conceals
A cavern; and through that a darksome way
Leads to the nether world; from which are heard
Dull sounds of voices, indistinct and awful;
And phantoms come and go with direful aspect;
That dreadful forms of living flames spring forth
To fasten on the mortal who may dare
Invade that secret place, and drag him thence,
Through horrid ranks of thronging, clutching fiends,
To Hades. Here Kaliphilus retires
To hold communion with familiar spirits,
And learn the secrets hid from mortal ken.
I tremble, and could not come near the place,
Had not my father given me this charm,

By him received from the dread master here,
To make approach unto this spot secure.
How shall I find him if he be within?
I dare not enter. I will call him forth.
Kaliphilus! What, ho! Kaliphilus!

ANTONIUS, *within.*

Who calls?

THONA.

'Tis not his voice!

ANTONIUS, *within.*

If thou art human
And on the earth would'st breathe the heavenly
air,
Come hither. Help me.

THONA.

Ah! what shall I do?
The door is fastened on the outer side;
Kaliphilus cannot then be within:
If that should be a voice to tempt me there
For my destruction.

ANTONIUS, *within.*

Come. Wilt thou not come?

THONA.

If it should be some mortal in distress —

ANTONIUS, *within.*

I pray thee help me.

THONA.

With this charm I 'm safe.

*Undoes the fastening of the door; Antonius discovered lying
bound upon the floor.*

ANTONIUS.

I thank thee, gentle — But art thou a spirit?

THONA.

I 'm only a weak girl.   And what art thou?

ANTONIUS.

An old man, as thou seest.   Pray unbind me.

THONA.

So.   Canst thou stand?

ANTONIUS.

Eh?   Yea.

THONA.

And walk?

ANTONIUS.

So, — so.

THONA.

Come forth into the air.

ANTONIUS.

Most willingly.

[*They come forth.*

THONA.

Thou art a Roman !

ANTONIUS.

I deny it not.

THONA.

Then wert thou safer in thy prison there.

ANTONIUS.

I seek not safety, but an open field,
And men, not spectres, for antagonists.

THONA.

What hast thou seen ?

ANTONIUS.

I know not — demons, ghosts,
And all the horrors necromancy leads.
The strangest dream — I know not if I wake.
Am I awake ? And art thou real?

THONA.

Ay, truly.

ANTONIUS.

Come, pinch me then. Why, yes, I think
    thou art real.
Thy little fingers sting — so fair a hand —
Sting me again; I 've been worse stung by
    kisses.
If I am not awake, my dream, now fair,
Makes me content to sleep.

THONA.

    How cam'st thou here ?

ANTONIUS.

A man, a great magician, as I think —

THONA.

Kaliphilus ?

ANTONIUS.

    'T was so I heard him called.
He found me shipwrecked, senseless on the
    shore ;
Restored my strength with simples ; brought me
    home,
And treated me with kindest courtesy ;
Protection offered me, and gave me food,
And entertained me with most wise discourse ;
Till from my story and his art he learned
That I a daughter had ; that she still lives.

Then, with incontinent persistence, he
Demanded her of me, which I refused.
Then passed a cloud upon his visage dark,
Which darker grew ; his muttered words fore-
    told
A storm. And so he left me ; soon returned ;
We were before his tent when last I saw him.
There, fixing his deep eyes on mine, he moved
His hands in gentle motion toward me, till
Unconsciousness possessed my every power,
And all since that is to me as a dream.
And when my senses, from their bonds es-
    caped,
'Gan take their watchful stations, and ere yet
I could persuade myself I did not dream,
I heard thy voice.

THONA.

        But he did not disarm thee ;
Thou hast thy sword.

ANTONIUS.

    A good and trusty friend.

THONA.

Thine armor and thy buckler thou may'st need.

ANTONIUS.

They should be near ; I left them in the sun.
So gentle, yet so brave — who art thou, girl ?

THONA.

My name is Thona.

ANTONIUS.

'T is a pretty name
Accordant with thyself.   Thou art native here ?

THONA.

Ay, to this clime.

ANTONIUS.

Thy mother was a lily.
A rose-tree surely was thy father.

THONA.

Nay,
My father is the druid chief.

ANTONIUS.

'T is well, —
A happy father.   I would have repose.
These limbs sustain a heavy weight of years,
And after such a dream I 'd dreamless rest.

THONA.

Come then with me unto a place of safety.
I have a friend will tender thee as well
As thine own daughter ; she is good to all.

Oh, thou shalt love her. She is happiest
When, by the magic of her tenderness,
She drives possessing powers of grief, and woe,
And weariness from sad, possessèd hearts,
And places there contentment.

ANTONIUS.

Who is she?

THONA.

A Roman captive.

ANTONIUS.

Bring me to her, then,
And have a sad and weary old man's thanks.

THONA.

Although a captive, she can care for thee
And make thee glad again. She will be glad
That I have brought thee; there thou shalt
        have rest.
Salome knoweth how —

ANTONIUS.

Salome!

THONA.

Yea,
Such is her name. Didst thou know her?

ANTONIUS.

Salome!
So was my daughter called.   I pray thee tell —
Know'st thou aught of her — whence she
came ?

THONA.

'T was she
Who asked John Baptist's head,— thou 'st heard
the tale ?

ANTONIUS.

No, no — it cannot be.   It cannot be.

THONA.

Wilt thou not lean on me ?   Thou art faint again.
Thy strength o'ertaxed —

ANTONIUS.

What was her mother's name?

THONA.

Herodias, the Queen —

ANTONIUS.

Ye gods!   Ye gods!
'T is she.

THONA.

What aileth thee ?   Alack!   he 's dead!

What have I done? O me! what shall I do?
No one to help me, all alone with him.

ANTONIUS.

Nay, let me sleep.

THONA.

He speaks! 'tis well! 'tis well!

ANTONIUS.

They told me that Salome lived again:
They did but mock me —

THONA.

Come, arouse thee. Come.

ANTONIUS.

The little stars danced in the East,
  And the little stars danced in the West,
When the Moon invited them all to a feast,
  But of all the bright dancers my love was
    the best.

THONA.

Who art thou?

ANTONIUS.

I? — I'll tell thee not. Away!

Did'st thou not say that thy name is Salome?
A sweet name and a dear. But she undid

The gates of evening, and went hence to light
The world beyond.   There shall we find her.
    Come.

THONA.

Nay, she is here.   And we will go to her.

ANOTNIUS.

I heard her calling to me in my dreams.
Her voice was like the music of the voices
Of many girls, when heard across the meadows.
I am Antonius, her father.

THONA.

Thou !

ANTONIUS.

I was her father, when I had a child :
Thou art not she — thou art like her, but not
    she.

THONA.

Art thou Antonius ?   Art thou her father ?

ANTONIUS.

I am Antonius.   J was her father.

THONA.

Oh joyful news !   But how to let her know,
So that too sudden joys, like heavenly fires

Too swift shot from the sky, blast not that
    life
Which they should gently warm into perfection.

ANTONIUS.

The owl said boo, and winked at the bat — ho,
    ho!
He did 't to fright me: in the dark we 're cow-
    ards.
He knows it.   Ah, how long and dark this
    night!

THONA.

Salome shall but place her hands on thee
And make thee well again.

ANTONIUS.

                    So?   Let us go.
But tell me, is Herodias still there?

THONA.

Nay, she is dead.

ANTONIUS.

    Why not?   Dead!   All are dead.

THONA.

Salome lives.   Shall we not go to her?

ANTONIUS.

Ah! I bethink me now.   My mind 's unsteady,
And changing breezes turn it from its course.
I am a ship hath sailed on many seas,
And been by wrathful storms so beat and
    wrecked,
So battered by cross-seas, so scathed by light-
    nings,
That, ballast lost, and rudder out of joint,
Each sudden gust can throw me helpless back,
Or drive me devious without pilotage.
My mind is old and worn, and easy crazed.

THONA.

Come, place thy hand upon my shoulder — so.
Dost thou feel stronger?

ANTONIUS.

Strong enough.   Let 's go.

A Garden before Alpindargo's House.

KALIPHILUS.

KALIPHILUS.

BRAVE Sextus caged ; Antonius secure,
So that, by chance, he shall not see Salome ;
His superstitious soul racked by my goblins
Till he shall have no strength to say me nay.
The subtle Ranmor favoring my plot,
For his revenge, but half conceiving it,
To be outwitted in the prosperous end,
And left to howl with rage.   She shall be mine.

Enter Salome.

I thank thee for this meeting, gentle friend.
When thou art hence a mocking troop of fears
Spring from my heart, like shadows from the
　　earth
When light is gone, and haunt my shivering
　soul ;
Which, terror stricken, waiteth for the dawn
Of thy bright coming through the dreary night,
Whose only light, thy cherished, kindly words,
Shining like stars in the dark firmament
Of memory, guides hope from death.   My days

Are marked by thine appearing and departure,
And all my world is by thy movements bounded,
As rising and down-going of the sun
Mark the out-circle of the sky's broad base.
Thoughts spring, when thou art away, as flowers
      in night,
Full of love fragrance and the dew of love.
And sighs, like shades heart-broken, then be-
      moan,
And words fast gather, like the birds at dawn,
Awaiting thine, as they the sun's approach,
To pour before thee gushing vows of love.

SALOME.

Why, thou hast told me this —

KALIPHILUS.

A thousand times.

SALOME.

And all thy varying phrase —

KALIPHILUS.

But says I love thee.

SALOME.

I would it were not so.

KALIPHILUS.
Oh, I so need
Thy love I needs must plead for it; though
thou
Should'st threaten thy displeasure, though I
knew
That I should cause thee torture, I must plead.
The tendrils of my heart have taken hold
Of thee; they twine and cling on every branch
And flower of thy soul. Where shall they fasten
If thou should'st throw them off? Where turn?
How rise?
Canst thou so push them from thee and not
break them?
Would'st thou with violence undo their grasp,
And my affections, which, with thee, aspire, —
Cast from thee, and, as vines without support,
Make them to grovel? When the storms of
passion
Sweep over them how shall they be o'er-
whelmed,
Crushed, and polluted!

SALOME.
Is a man so weak?

KALIPHILUS.
It is not weakness; it is strength,—such strength

As will not be resisted ; such as piles
Ossa on Pelion and climbs to heaven.

SALOME.

A pine were weak which so should lean upon
A weeping willow, or an aspen-tree.

KALIPHILUS.

But vines from soil too rich and powerful
Which climb, and clasp, and bend the tallest tops
Of most disdainful trees, and cover them,
And make them but the frames to which they
   cling,
Investing them with their own flowering beau-
   ties, —
Such are not weak, and such are my affections.
Yet may their panting foliage be held up
By even a frail and trembling support.
But if that fail them, or they have it not,
They roll in stained exuberance on the earth,
Their purity all gone, as is a wave's
When o'er its bounds it breaks, and on the
   ground
Runs stumbling.

SALOME.

   Is 't my pity thou would'st have ?
'T is thine. I never so did pity man.

KALIPHILUS.

Nay, pity is but half of love — its part
Unselfish; fix thy selfish love on me
So that I be the other part of thee, —
The part least worthy, but the most beloved,
The ward and warden of thy happiness.

SALOME.

With pity, then, the holier half of love,
And gratitude, I pray thee be content.

KALIPHILUS.

But pity ever grows by its own action,
And often from it springs, feebly at first,
The other, selfish part of perfect love.
I 'd have such love of thee ; so pity me.

SALOME.

I cannot love thee: urge me then no more.

KALIPHILUS.

But thou must love me ; do not say me nay.
I cannot go without thee ; cannot stay
Here with thee ; I must go, must go, must go.
I cannot die, alas ! I cannot die !
If I could die, I 'd sever now the bonds
Which bind thee to me, and as mine own
    ghost,
Surrender thee and go to darkness.

SALOME.

Hush!

KALIPHILUS.

Behold! the flocks of swooping torments cloud
The light, and plane above me; in the air
I hear the hissing of the driving scourge,
Which, me pursuing, comes again apace.
I go. Ere yet the martial morn shall bear
Its purple standard up the eastern slope
Of heaven, I must depart. Extend thy love,
As a protecting angel spreads its wings
Around, to shelter me.

SALOME.

I cannot love thee.
My heart begins to fear, and shrink from thee:
Thy face is changed, and anguish comes upon
    it,
Such as the fallen Lucifer might bear.

KALIPHILUS.

The anguish of my love kept from its own.

SALOME.

Its own?

KALIPHILUS.

Yea, I have earned the right to own thee.

I 've bought thee with my soul. Then of my
    soul
Take thou the place.

SALOME.

        Alas! a sinful soul
Wouldst thou have then.

KALIPHILUS.

       Thou dost not know me yet.
I saw thee dance before King Herod; loved;
Heard thy demand for John the Baptist's head.
And, when the executioner refused,
For that in him some throbs of nature moved,
To do his office on the holy man,
I took his place, because it was thy wish
To have that head.

SALOME.

    O spare me. Speak not of it.

KALIPHILUS.

Thou tremblest. Sooner I 'd have gone to hell
To lead the devil chained, had I but known
What was before me; sooner would have met
The roaring fiends in phalanx than his look,
Though full of tenderness and pity, or
Have heard his voice, as he was praying for
    me.

And, when the axe fell on his spotless neck,
A light celestial filled the dungeon; forms
Of heavenly beauty floated in the air,
And seemed to lift the prison roof and pass
Into the skies. I brought the head to thee,
And saw thy horror; saw thee swoon, and fled,
Lest thou should'st wake and curse me.

SALOME.

O my God!

Is it not finished!

KALIPHILUS.

Then returned, a courtier,
I sought thee through the palace, but in vain.
Two fires consumed me: passion, lit by thee;
Remorse, for slaying him.

SALOME.

O pity me!

KALIPHILUS.

The thousand telescopic eyes of power,
From its bright eminence, could see thee not,
Though ranging all the world, and hopelessly
My passion groped. I could not bear the weight
Of my remorse, which crushed me, whispering
ever

That I had killed a prophet of my people.
To make amends, a zealot I became
For the old religion; ignorant that he,
Whom I had slain, came to announce its end.
So, when the Christ was brought to trial, none
Cried out so loud as I to crucify Him.
I thought I did God service. I had read
The prophets, but I understood them not.
I waited still a Christ more glorious
Than Solomon; than David more inspired;
And, when they led Him forth to execution,
Whom I believed impostor and blasphemer,
And He was fainting underneath His cross,
And moved but slowly, with unsteady step,
Spurred, as I thought, by a most holy zeal,
I smote Him with my open hand, and said, —
Go faster. Instant with the stroke I felt
A weariness, as of a thousand years,
Which cleft my bones, my marrow melted, crushed
My firm-knit muscles, cracked each separate nerve,
As He looked on me, terrible as God
In judgment; while, with voice unheard by others,
To me as awful as that which shall yet
Pronounce the final sentence, He declared

My doom, — to walk the earth until that day
When He as final judge shall come again.

SALOME.

Oh, dreadful !

KALIPHILUS.

     Through my frame great terror ran,
And Hell came surging o'er me ; everywhere
Its mounting billows boiled, while awful gulfs
Lay dark and bottomless between.

SALOME.

                Poor soul !

KALIPHILUS.

The rude procession passed. I turned and fled,
Surprised that I could flee not overwhelmed,
And find what seemed the earth still under me.
While thunders followed after me and cried,
As if about to alight upon my shoulders, —
Go faster, Jew ; go faster.

SALOME.

             Hopeless Jew !

KALIPHILUS.

I am so weary ! I have wandered now
For what should be ten thousand centuries,
And yet I count the years upon my fingers.
And so to wander wearily forever !

Why e'en the stars, which seem eternal, fall,
As fruits mature, from heaven's silver tree,
And cease to be. How sweetly then they rest!
But I shall never ripen, ne'er decay.
Shall live till one by one they all fall down,
And the great dome, like to a withered top
Of an o'eragèd pine when fire is set
Among its branches, disappear in flames.
Oh, I should pity them, if they, like me,
Must wander on forever in the night,
Growing so old, and yet forever young;
The bloom which they first looked upon all
    faded;
The valleys, where, in their young life, they
    kept
Love-vigils and the appointments sweet of love,
Long turned to deserts, where lie branch and
    trunk
Of trees which blushed and trembled in their
    gaze,
Gnawed bare by the devouring years, and
    bleached
Like bones of a long-perished caravan.
How weary must they be of shining then
When they shall know they shine for none
    they 've loved.

SALOME.

Oh I do pity thee.

KALIPHILUS.

Dost thou indeed ?
Since here I found thee I have had some res-
　　pite, —
And that dread voice has ceased to drive me on.
The dreadful weariness shall recommence,
The scourge shall fall, the voice shall make me
　　quake,
So soon as thou shalt leave me.

SALOME.

Oh, alas !

KALIPHILUS.

This respite is the fruit of love for thee ;
For love is Heaven, and Heaven is perfect
　　rest.
Save thee I hate all things, and hate is Hell.
So thou for me art Heaven, my only hope.
Thy lips for me the gates of Paradise,
Thine eyes the crystal sea, thy brow the throne,
Thy hair the darkness overshadowing it.
Shall I not plead for thee, as thou wouldst plead
For thy salvation ?　Shall I not be heard,
As thou wouldst be by Him who holds the
　　keys
Of the celestial city ?　Wouldst thou not
By will persistent climb the way to heaven,
And enter it by force, and capture there

Redemption, rather than be cast away?
So will I plead, so climb, so capture thee,
My heaven. There 's majesty in the true love
Of a true man compels a mutual love;
It should not plead, but gently overcome.

SALOME.

I cannot love thee.   Would that I could help
  thee.
My heart bleeds for thee.   Wilt thou not re-
  pent?
There's nothing hopeless but impenitence,
Repent, and be forgiven.

KALIPHILUS.

                    I have dared,
And felt damnation for thee, and would still
In hell be happy, if thou wouldst but love me.
I bear no marks, such as the devils have,
Put on them in their prison-house, to bear
Forever; I come not and vanish; no,
Nor enter into men.   Yet I 'm a devil,
And burn in tortures; plot, and hate, and
  mock.
Whichever way I go I wade in torments.
And this for thee.   Can such as I repent
And ask forgiveness?   Could I rise to heaven,

10

E'en to its crystal gates the flames would
    burn
With tenfold torture. Though I went beyond
The farthest flight of morn's far‑shooting ar‑
    rows,
The horrid pit would seethe around me still.
I bear it in me — a whole universe
Of woe.

SALOME.

I 'll pray for thee; mayhap He 'll hear.

KALIPHILUS.

He will not hear thee ; or will hear to laugh.
Nay, I cannot repent; 't is His decree.
For, could I once repent, He must forgive,
Since He hath so professed, and cannot lie.
Forgiveness were the end of this my woe ;
And so my punishment were ended ; so
His judgment made of no effect. Ah no.
I am not in a state of trial, but
Of retribution. My probation 's ended.
He dare not pardon me ; nay, ask Him not ;
He cannot do it.

SALOME.

Pray thee, speak not so.

KALIPHILUS.

I will blaspheme and curse Him. I will tempt,

That He, perchance, may blow upon and blast
    me.
I will dishonor Him in His own image ;
I 'll prove that He, assuming all perfections,
Hath made a devil in His glorious form,
Permits him, nay, doth bait and tempt him on.

SALOME.

The phrases from thy strong, o'erheated soul
Like dark clouds rise, in which the thunder
    rides
Concealed. I pray thee be more calm. I fear
The threatened bolts. Argue more patiently.

KALIPHILUS.

Fie ! Bid the surface of the infernal lake
Be calm while all its fires are leaping; ask
Tornadoes but to whisper in thine ear
Like zephyrs ; or the thunder-storm to speak
In tones like those of a love-making boy.
If they obey thee, then will I o'ercome
The boiling tumult in my soul, and be
A kneeling, soft-toned pleader, smooth and calm.

SALOME.

But, if thy vaulting words so strike at Heaven,
I 'll hear thee not.

KALIPHILUS.

Omnipotence itself
Cannot undo my doom, nor add thereto.
It cannot blot me out; that would be bliss.
Nor add unto my woe, for that would end me.
Thou art my only hope, my holiness.
Let, then, thy love be as a draught, to cool,
If but a moment, this consuming torment;
A drop upon my parching tongue; a breath
Of heaven's air, in death to give me life;
A hand to stay me as I sink forever;
A draught, in which, from thy bright soul as
        from
A crystal cup filled at the fount of hope,
Held by an angel from the throne of God,
I 'd drink eternal life.

SALOME.

Would it were thine!
Thy love for me can never make thee blest;
Nor mine for thee, though I should love thee
        more
Than thine own wish could name, if powerful
To grasp and wield the perfect language, which
Pure spirits in communion use. The love
Of Him, whom thou hast wounded, can alone
Make thee forever happy. Seek it then.

KALIPHILUS.

I am condemned, therefore cannot repent.
For, if in hell the devils could repent,
And be forgiven, the arch fiend himself
Were but a sinner, not a hopeless devil.
'T is sin and condemnation makes the fiend ;
The awful fiat of the final doom,
Irrevocable, making sin eternal,
Destroying wholly sweet forgetfulness,
And kindling memory to a burning lake.
Alas, alas, that I could hope for death !

SALOME.

Yea, death may be unto the lowly saint
A rose-clad portal, though the dreaded gate
By which all throng into an unknown land.

KALIPHILUS.

But let it rise before me in its form
In which all terrors mingle indistinct,
And glare from eyeless sockets burning dull ;
With suffocating darkness fill the world,
Breathed from its nostrils ; while beneath I feel
Long arms upreaching, folding me about,
To drag me down the bottomless abyss,
Which opens under me ; ay, let him seize
Each separate nerve, in all its trembling parts,
With red-hot, gnawing pincers which consume
    not,

And hold me in them o'er a reeking gulf,
With horrors roaring, where the dashing wrecks
Of lost worlds, crashing in the fiery sea,
Mingle their dull reports with shrieks and jeers,
And groans, and laughs infernal, till his arms,
His hundred thousand never tiring arms,
Shall all grow weary, and I 'll welcome him
With rapture, on him fix a lover's grasp,
If, after all, he will but blot me out,
So that nor memory, nor consciousness,
Nor fear, nor dread, nor any thing am I.

SALOME.

What misery is thine! "Come unto me
Ye who are heavy laden, I will give
You rest." So hath the Master promised; come,
Oh, come to Him.

KALIPHILUS.

I cannot, will not, — no,
Though He should come and here beseech me; no.
How could I know Him that He was the Christ?
He made me what I am, and makes me wish
To be so, rather than before Him bow
In penitence. Such is my condemnation.
I would be penitent to thwart His will
If it were possible; but He 's Almighty.
Heed thou my prayer. His lightnings I 've
    outfaced,

But worship thee, as I, in days of yore,
Before Jehovah bowed and made confession,
While yet the Lord of Israel was my God.

SALOME.

I cannot listen to thee. Cease, I pray.
What profit hast thou so to wound my soul,
And make me see how very bad thou art?

KALIPHILUS.

I must lay bare my parching, burning heart,
And let the gentle dew of sweet confession
Upon it fall. And so I come to thee
And open all my life. I would be known
By thee as by myself; 't is love's demand,
And tender proof of love. I know that thou
Hast tenderness and mercy like His own,
Without His vengeance and His dreadful justice;
And I would feel thy soul envelop me,
As holiness of God enfolds His saints.
The story of my sins awakes thy pity,
And leads it to me weeping, as I lie
Before thee prostrate. Pity leads thy thoughts;
Thy thoughts shall silently lead forward love,
Who, blind, is always led, and I be blest.

SALOME.

Thou 'dst have me love him who hath done
those things

My soul abhors ? Could I speak thus to thee ? —
I know thou art not good, and yet I love thee ;
I know thou art not faithful, yet I love thee ;
I know thou art most sinful, yet I love thee ;
I will not say I love thee for thy sinning,
But yet thy sinning makes me love thee more, —
Should I speak thus to thee ?

KALIPHILUS.

                    Ay, ay, forever.
And that were womanlike.

SALOME.

                  Perchance it were.

KALIPHILUS.

So love me, and my sinning shall be o'er,
And memory shall be awhile beguiled
Of half its terrors, which now haunt my soul,
More dread than those which dwell beneath the
    world,
Where Lucifer rides roaring on the ruin,
Drives on the storms, and works the general
    wreck.

SALOME.

If thou couldst pray —

KALIPHILUS.

             I could create myself,

For I could sooner breathe the breath of life
Into a soul than prayer into my heart.

SALOME.

Nay, turn thy thoughts to holy things and hope ;
Thy brain is heated till its vapors form
Unreal and dreadful shapes. Thy love for me
Shall pass away with them. The sun which
     makes
The vapors rise from earth dispels them too.

KALIPHILUS.

By the great devil I swear ; by his black throne
Fast anchored where huge fire-billows break,
From every seething side, forever on it;
And by the pitchy dome, the groans which surge
Above the bellowing of the flaming tides,
The whole affection of my passionate soul
Is fixed upon thee, never can be moved.

SALOME.

Oh, swear not such an oath !

KALIPHILUS.

              I 'll swear by thee,
Sole good, sole hope, sole deity for me.

SALOME.

Thou shalt not call me so.   I will not hear thee ;
Thou shalt no more so use me to blaspheme.

KALIPHILUS.

See how I need the sweet dew of thy love
To cool this torment, calm this raging woe.

SALOME.

Come with me ; let me pray for thee and me.

KALIPHILUS.

I will not hear thee till thou grant my prayer.
Nay, leave this savage isle, and come with me
Upon these waters to some land not cursed.
I will unlock the stars, and we will go
Beyond their glittering barriers, beyond
The western portals of the firmament —

SALOME.

I cannot go with thee ; entreat me not.

KALIPHILUS.

Where, as from chaos, will I call a world,
Which, hidden, lies there richer than the
        thoughts
Of eastern dreamers, sleeping where the sun
Selects his golden rays ; so very fair

As it were made for thine abode ; so great
As 't were the cradle and the home of giants.
And we will be its Adam and its Eve,
Its patriarchs, its prophets, king and queen.

SALOME.

My duty binds me here to this poor people.
But could I leave them in their utmost need,
And could I love thee, I could never go
Under the guidance of so wild a vision.

KALIPHILUS.

So were the holy prophets' visions scorned,
Foreshadowing no purer truth than this.

SALOME.

Oh, mock not at their holiness.

KALIPHILUS.

Not I.
The devil himself can truly prophesy,
And I, unholy, still may speak the truth.
Why, know'st thou not, girl, that the only thing
About me holy is my love for thee ? —
The only purifier, only savior, —
And that it, like a glory, emanates
And wraps me round, and makes me like a god

In nobleness, in purity, in strength,
When I am with thee, hoping that thou 'lt
   love me?

SALOME.

Oh, seek a higher holiness, a love
That lasts for aye. For mine thou must not
   hope.

KALIPHILUS.

Strip not the archangel of his glory, lest
He leave his place and roam a naked fiend.

SALOME.

If thou wilt not pray I will pray alone,
And, with thine, bring my woes before the
   Throne.

A Sacred Grove near the Sea-shore.

DRUIDS, BARDS, AND WARRIORS.

DRUIDS.

HEAR the shouting waters!
Every wave, a courier, brings
News portentous, cries of slaughters,
  Each to outstrip the other, springs.
On the shore each, falling breathless,
  Faints ere foaming lips can utter
Warning words of import deathless,
  Yet, of foes approaching mutter.

BARDS.

To the trees the swift south winds
  Whisper mysteries, as they go,
And the sacred grove unbinds
  Chaplets of the mistletoe,
Casts them to the flying breeze,
Bending toward it as it flees.
And the oaks, unused to fly,
Lift their branches to the sky,
As, in terror, hands on high
Are lifted deprecatingly,

For defense from woes to be,
Coming from the southern sea.

WARRIORS.

The king of the world refits his ships !
His horses dash on with foam-flinging lips !
　As the rays of the sun,
Our spears in the fame-giving rush of the fight
Shall scatter this brooding cloud of night
　Ere the day be done !

A BARD.

Behold ! the king approaches !

Enter CARACTACUS.

DRUIDS.

All hail, Caractacus !

BARDS.

Hail, king of British men !

WARRIORS.

All hail, thou chief of warriors !

CARACTACUS.

In days gone by our fields were clothed in
　　green
Our forests ever singing hymns to Peace,

Our brooks made music for the dancing flowers.
Our daughters wandered, safe as goddesses,
Through all the sylvan labyrinths, and sought
Upon the sea-shore, in the quiet glen,
Or on the mountain side, or in the lake,
The chaste embrace of health, and as they
    blushed,
Quick modesty with crimson banners came,
And o'er the plains and hills of each sweet
    face,
And dimpled valleys, where their smiles lay
    hid,
With health contested for the mastery.
And as they chased each other o'er the field
Now banners of the one, the other's now
Were up and down. And in each peaceful bay
The heavens gathered undisturbed their brood
Of clouds reflected. Then to peaceful vales
The kine went forth at morn, again at eve
To come securely back. In waving fields
Unguarded stayed the harvest for the hand
Which had prepared it. From the mountain
    glen
Then came the hunter home full sure to find
His treasures safe ; that no intrusive tread
Had visited the temple of his love.
His weapons on the wall in order hung ;
He lay at ease, the while his gentle mate

With busy gladness, and the quiet joy
Of strong affection with its all content,
Moved lightly to prepare the evening meal;
Still talking of the children, of their sports,
Their wondrous sayings, their precocious lore;
Or of the visits from her neighbors fair,
Or marvelous story from some gossip heard.
The supper ended, every dish disposed
In orderly array upon their shelves,
With door unbarred, they seek their waiting
    couch,
Nor think of guard, but trust their sole defense
To their own honesty and innocence.

DRUIDS.

'T was so.   Ah, calm, religious days!

BARDS.

'T was so.   Ah, beauteous, happy days!

WARRIORS.

'T was so.   Ah, dull and heavy days!

CARACTACUS.

The king of the world arose,
He summoned his Roman hosts.
He lifted up the spear,
He mounts his wave-borne coursers.

The south wind guides him to our shore.
Bright his gleaming steel,
Strange his engines,
Strong his shields,
Stern his warriors,
Terrible his showers of death.
Our young men fall.
His host leaps on our strand.
Our virgins are made captives;
Dreadfully, by distant breezes borne,
We hear their fainting wail.
Our houses flame,
Downtrodden are our fields,
Our harvests by the stranger gathered,
Our wives defiled,
Our children fatherless,
Our sacred groves polluted,
Our crystal fountains turned to blood.
Ghosts sadly wander by our streams;
Mourning spirits, walking on our hills
In misty robes, are seen.
Orbèd comets drive athwart the skies,
Before so peaceful.
Fiery dust, in ever-lengthening clouds,
Marks their headlong course.

DRUIDS.

Why sleep ye, gods of Briton?

Awake, awake!
Come from your airy halls.

WARRIORS.

Strike the shield.
Rouse the heroes;
Raise the song, ye Bards.

BARDS.

Our harps are sad;
They will not utter a defiant measure;
They tremble and lament.

CARACTACUS.

The king of the world hath wrought this change.
The gods of Rome exult.
Where our warriors?
Where our men of old?
Their ghosts came joyously on clouds
To see the fight.
They thought again to see
The deeds of old.
They saw their weak-armed sons.
They saw their timid children fail.
They turned away,
They hid their faces in their cloudy mantles,
And mournfully returned into their place.
Where were our men of old?
Where were our warriors?

WARRIORS.

Our warriors met the foe.
They were not timid ;
They were not weak armed.
The stranger's host was many ;
They were few. —
Smite the shield,
Bear the challenge forth,
Bid the wave-borne stranger come again.

CARACTACUS.

Two times hath Bel performed his daily course
And carried his bright shield,
Light-giving, through the heavens, since again
The ship-borne Romans on the flood were seen.
Their burnished armor, on the enridgèd sea
Flashed warnings,
As beacon-fires upon our mountain ranges.
Again with fear and joy
Our trembling maidens saw
Our youthful warriors assume their arms,
And hoped, with timid doubts,
To see them with their fame return.
Again in dim array
Our fathers' ghosts assembled on the clouds,
But slowly and with sadness,
Lest they once more should see
Their feeble sons retire.

WARRIORS.

Feeble are not their sons.
The spear was uplifted,
The sword of our fathers unsheathed;
The boastful foe came not.

CARACTACUS.

Vainly looked the ghosts.
The maidens feared and hoped in vain.
Bright dwellers in the airy halls had seen
Our haughty island lashed
Before the stranger's face.
They could not see it lashed again.
The men of old were dead, —
The heroes of the times of old;
And there were none to guard it, —
No heroes to repel the insulting foe.
Then came the gods from cloudy palaces
Swift-riding on the storms,
In panoply of fire.
The waters prostrate fell
Upon the sand.
The forest bowed itself.
They breathed upon the proud, sea-ruling host;
With thundering noise the ponderous locks they
      turned,
And from their cages let the raging winds.
Then melted all the stranger's ships,

And disappeared as mists.
His warriors,
Like stones hurled on the billows, sunk.
The king of the world
Looks from his lofty tower :
He scans the north way for his conquering hosts
Returning.
They come not.
Wearied is he gazing,
But they come not.
Bright eyes of their women now grow · dim,
Like the moon when mists arise,
For they look through tears
Vainly for their loved ones.
But our maidens' eyes are like the sun
After showers.
In their rays some drops still glisten,
For they see their warriors
With shining arms and spears not reddened
Returning
Without their fame ;
Not heroes.
The gods of Briton overthrew
Unaided these proud Romans.

Enter RANMOR.

RANMOR.

Where are the priests ?
Where is the sacrifice ?

Who bringeth a thank-offering?
What! shall our gods be mocked?
Where is the sacrifice?
Where are the priests?

DRUIDS.

The priests attend.
They do not mock the gods.
They have no Roman captive
A victim for the sacrifice.
To offer any other were
To mock the gods.

CARACTACUS.

Ye have no captive!
Hush! proclaim it not.
The warriors of the times of old
Shall hear, and leave the feast of shells
To lift the shadowy spear,
Or wander mourning in their native vales.
Where are thy warriors, Briton?
Thy maidens follow in the stranger's triumph.
Thou hast no captive!
Thy virgins spread the couch for Roman mas-
        ters.
Thou hast no captive!
Thy wailing wives make joyous the world's
        king.

Thou hast no captive !
Where are thy warriors, Briton ?
Where thy heroes' fame ?
Where is thy glory ?
Where is thy defense ?
Thy women shall lift up the spear,
Shall draw the bow, and handle the bossed
    buckler.
Thy men have failed.
Where are thy warriors, Briton ? —

Enter a MESSENGER.

What news ?

MESSENGER.

    Upon the southern sea a force
Of many ships, as flocks of water-fowl,
Are seen ; their numbers growing ; one by one
They seem to alight upon the swelling main.

CARACTACUS.

The king of ships is on his course.
His wingèd steeds are harnessed.
They prance along the main.
Their foaming breasts defy us.

MESSENGER.

They yet are distant, and the peevish winds
Now turn against them —

CARACTACUS.

Ere they come
We can prepare a sacrifice,
Appease the gods,
New whet the sword and spear —

DRUIDS.

Behold the chief!

BARDS.

Lo! Alpindargo comes — the Just.

WARRIORS.

The holy Alpindargo shall instruct us.

Enter ALPINDARGO.

ALPINDARGO.

Peace be with you, my children.

CARACTACUS.

Peace? When the eagles from their heights
    descend,
The hawks are screaming, and the wolves are
    howling?
The stranger cometh with his ships.

ALPINDARGO.

I know it.

CARACTACUS.

What shall we do?

ALPINDARGO.

Resist him.
Were this a question of aggressive war
Brave men might differ. Who would not de-
    fend
His home against invaders unprovoked
Should lose the name of Briton: let him go
And take his place with the invaders' slaves,
And a new name. Else must he faint and
    die,
For British air can never nourish cowards.
Within a thousand halls the men, whose words
Live after them, have told you how your sires
Met the ship-driving foe and vanquished him;
How mighty were their spears in hands of heroes.
Have any sucked the milk of hares, to say, —
Come, let us flee? Let them as hares be
    hunted.
Were any cradled in a serpent's nest
And abject taught to crawl? Then let them
    hiss,
And abject crawl out of the ranks of men.
Would any lay aside the shield and spear
To sing of peace, and do a master's bidding?
Go, come, as he commands, — eat, drink, and
    sleep,

As he permits ? Let him go serve their women ;
For such were made to serve, but not in
    Briton.
Those who would dwell in Briton must be
    masters,   .
Subjected never ; British men must rule.
Who talks of prudence ? What is prudence,
    then ?
To tamely serve insulting foes ? or choose
That way which leads to mastery or death ?
If mastery — then freedom, wealth, and peace,
The love and grateful honor of our children.
If death — fame, glory in the halls of Hesus.

WARRIORS.

Call the wolves ! Call the hawks ? Call crows
    and ravens !
Let Slaughter bid his guests.
Death to all foes ! double death to all cravens !
We wait our chief's behests.

BARDS.

Let the king of the world
Come on with his ship-borne hosts !
Ere the banners of morn be unfurled
They shall wander, bewailing ghosts.
Ho, ho, for the battle !
The clangor of shields and the arrows' swift
    rattle !

DRUIDS.

The sacrifice ! the sacrifice ! else we offend the
    gods !
Our gods offended are our foes' allies.
Vain, then, our valor; vain our prayers and
    cries ;
Nor spear, nor buckler, can avail against so
    dreadful odds.

CARACTACUS.

Tell us, holy man,
The battle's issue.

ALPINDARGO.

I come now from the mount of vision,
From which I saw what shall be
If we propitiate the gods.
Jow, looking from his cloudy halls, beheld
Upon the horizon's southern verge approach
A form which darkened all the heavens, and
    knew
The earth-quaking tread of Mars. Jow calls
    Taranis ;
And fast, loud breathing, from his darksome
    cave
The god swells out and scans the darkened sky.
He sees swift-moving Mars, whose mantle black
A bloody border marks, and forms of ruin,

And conflagrations run along its edge.
And now the gods both hear his distant chal-
    lenge, —
A roar reverberating through the arch,
On which the yet unshaken heavens rest,
Deep as the ocean's opening cry, when first
The south-west wind disturbs its heavy slum-
    bers.
With answering roar Jow threw the challenge
    back.
Then shook the earth, and many stars, dis-
    placed,
Fell hissing in the sea, which boiled with heat.
One foot upon a tower of eastern clouds,
One on a cloud-built mountain in the west,
Taranis stands, and lifts his form on high,
Prepared to summon all the gods to war.
His mantle falls, like night, upon the earth ;
His breath beclouds the heavens. He firmly
    grasps
His awful sledge, swings it from pole to pole,
Swift gleaming like a comet in the dark,
And smites the shield carried aloft by Bel,
Whose rays illumine all the universe.
From its just equipoise by the fierce blow
It swings, and shivering with loud outcry
Gives forth resounding thunders ; and the orbs
In their remotest rounds shake at their posts.

Its rim of rays, all shattered by the stroke,
Fall, glancing lightnings, through the darkened
    air.
Swifter and fiercer fall the dreadful blows,
Swifter and fiercer flash the lightnings down,
In darker volumes rolls his surging breath,
With deeper clangor rolls the thunderous call.
By labor heated, from his hidden brows
Fall steaming showers, deluging the earth.
From every quarter rush the gods in arms,
Demand the cause of the alarm, and stand
In dread array on cloudy battlements.
Teutates first advances to the front
And shouts defiance to the frowning foe ;
But Hesus laughs, exulting, and stands forth,
And claims his right eternal to conduct
The fight. The yielding gods stand back in awe.
He rushes forward in mid-air to meet
Mars, moving on apace, with roar defiant.
And quickly, from their mouths, black clouds
    of smoke
Envelop them, and nothing can be seen
But awful surge of darkness overhead,
And dazzling flash of blazing sword thrusts
    through
The rent concealment; nothing can be heard
But their commingling roars, which shake the
    earth,

The shock of their orbed shields and armors'
    clash.
From north to south, from east to west, through
    all
The hemisphere the battle raged till Mars,
His crest shorn off, his great shield cleft in
    twain,
Retreated to the East, and there held up,
In sign of peace, above his drooping head,
A banner barred with seven colors bright
Which spanned the firmament. The gods with-
    drew,
The darkness vanished, and the heavens smiled.
So, from the mount of vision, I beheld
The war, and triumph of our British gods.
As Mars was driven to his old domain,
So from these western isles the invading host
Of Latin races shall be driven back
To their old fastnesses and dreams of rule.
  O Britain, sea-borne queen,
  Thou ruler of the waters,
  Waken thy heroes.
  Call them with the voice of thy waves;
  Let them show thy youths the ways of fame,
  And lead them in battle.
  Thy head must not be bent —
  Peerless among the isles;
  No fetters mark thy wrists,

No chains thy ankles ;
Naught but thy sea-foam diadem
Shall e'er constrain thee.
Be all thy goings
Free as thy breath of winds.

RANMOR.

Friends, ye have heard great Alpindargo speak.
His words are good, such as he always utters.
A victory he promises if we
Propitiate the gods. Shall we not do it ?
But, said Caractacus, we have no captive,
And so no victim. How then shall we make
Propitiation ? Alpindargo saith,
Propitiate the gods and ye shall triumph.
But Alpindargo hath prepared no victim ;
And Alpindargo is our holy chief.
Without a victim no propitiation ;
Without propitiation sure defeat ;
And with defeat —

WARRIORS.

Nay, nay, it shall not be.

RANMOR.

Bards, Druids, Warriors, be it known to you
That, harbored in this isle, a Roman captive
Hath dwelt in safety, favored by the king,
By Alpindargo, and the great magician.

WARRIORS.

Where is he ?   Bring him forth.

DRUIDS.

Ay, bring him forth.

RANMOR.

Yet, Warriors, the king reproaches you,
And asks a victim for the sacrifice.
Yet, O ye Druids, Alpindargo mocks you,
And brings no victim for the sacrifice.

DRUIDS.

He shall not mock us.

WARRIORS.

Bring the captive forth.

RANMOR.

It is well known to you, O holy Druids,
Who keep the mysteries of the eternal gods,
And are the interpreters of their great wills ; —
Well known to you, O learned and reverend
          Bards,
Who are the tongues of present time, who
          guard
The echoing voices of the years long passed ;
Who send the voice of Now through years to
          come,

And are the judgments, and the mouths of
    Fame ; —
Well known to you, brave Warriors, who stand
As Briton's cliffs to meet the assaulting waves
Of enemies, unshaken, and have heard
From year to year the mighty deeds rehearsed
Which made the glory of your hero-fathers, —
This is the day of annual sacrifice.
Ye have been well instructed ;—the Arch-Druid,
The holy Alpindargo, loves his people,
And hath them well instructed ; — well ye know
The oracle brought to us from the gods, —

When this sacrifice shall fail,
Britons shall their priests bewail;

That if we would propitiate the Heavens
This offering must be made ; that else, the gods
In wrath shall surely let our foes prevail.
Yet Alpindargo keeps the victim hid ;
Yet King Caractacus protects the captive.
Remember too, the great deliverance
But yesterday wrought for us by the gods,
When, with their misty steeds, they rode upon
The waters, treading underfoot the ships,
And hurling warriors to the sea's abyss.
So went the gods before, and left for you
No captives, O brave Warriors. Yet the king
Asks you for captives ; chides you that ye took

12

No captives. Alpindargo comes, O Druids,
To tell you what the gods shall do, if you
Provide a victim, while he still conceals
The only Roman captive —

DRUIDS AND WARRIORS.

Bring him forth.

RANMOR.

Ye know, O friends, — I speak thus but in duty ;
For where religion and my country calls
I were a recreant if I failed to hear, —
A twofold recreant if I failed to speak, —
Ye know where ye may find a king to rule,
A priest to serve, but never to deceive you.

CARACTACUS.

Name thou the captive, O disloyal priest.

RANMOR.

Forgettest thou Salome,
Perverter of religion,
Contemner of the gods,
Opposer of the sacrifices ?

CARACTACUS.

Nay, she hath been long here
A ministrant in sorrow to our people,
And should no more be called a captive.

RANMOR.

She is a captive of the Roman race —
The gods demand her.

DRUIDS.

Ay, the gods demand her.

BARDS.

Must that flower fade ?
Shall that rose-tree fall
Filled with blossoms ?
Must its head be low ?

RANMOR.

What saith the holy Alpindargo ?   What
Our sacred chief who careth for his people ?

ALPINDARGO.

I know thee, godless priest.
I know thy vain ambition,
I know thy perjured faith,
I know thy spotted heart.
Couldst thou not wait yet a few days or months,
Till, in the natural progress of decay,
Like an o'er-aged tree, whose sappy founts
Are dry, I fall and leave a vacant place,
That thou shouldst seek to undermine my roots,
And headlong hurry to transplant thyself

To where I stand, if so thy peers permit?
Not veneration for the mighty gods,
Not tenderness for thy endangered country, —
Ambition and revenge impel thy speech.
I know the impious purposes
With which thou didst pursue the captive;
How thou didst wither in her scorn,
Cringe back before her virtue,
As wolves before the face of fire ;
I know thy subtlety.
I know thy groveling thoughts,
Thy too aspiring pride.
I know thy vengeful soul,
Ay, recreant priest, I know thee.
Stand back, for shame, blasphemer :
The gods would not accept thy sacrifice.

RANMOR.

Druids, demand the sacrifice.

DRUIDS.

The sacrifice ! the sacrifice !
When this sacrifice shall fail,
Britons shall their priests bewail.

ALPINDARGO.

Brothers and friends, and thou, audacious
    priest,

I too were recreant if any thing —
Ease, honors, life — could be more dear to me
Than service of the gods, and all the rites.
Of our religion ; and a traitor I,
Were mine own flesh and blood to me more dear
Than my dear land. Ye know how I have
    loved,
E'en as a father loveth his own child,
This unprotected captive, whose pure life
And constant acts of noble charity,
Though guided by false faith, might shame us
    all.
But now the gods demand her at my hand,
And I must not withhold her ; now our country
Requires her blood, I must not hold it back.
Let her be offered as the sacrifice.

CARACTACUS.

We cannot take her, for Kaliphilus —

ALPINDARGO.

The gods are stronger than Kaliphilus.

RANMOR.

But he will yield her ; he hath told me so. —
Go, some of you, and take her ; bind her fast —

ALPINDARGO.

Hold! Lay no hand upon her till the hour
Of sacrifice, when, on the sunset tide,
The evening breeze is moving to the vales.
With reverence then attend, and bring her here,
Gently as shadows lead the Queen of Night.

RANMOR.

But, meanwhile, post your guards that she escape not.

CARACTACUS.

Bards, lift the song, for heaviness is on me, —
The song which leadeth forth the souls of heroes.

BARDS.

The ghosts of the silent years go past,
  Their snowy robes are dim and long;
They whisper to us and vanish fast, —
  They whisper to us the words of this song:

The Northman came from his hill,
  Bright was his leveled spear;
The sound of the harping was still,
  While his voice cried loud and clear, —
Come every hawk from the air,
  And take for his famishing brood;
Come every wolf from his lair,
  And drink from the rivers of blood.

Then Casivel rose from his place,
　At the head of the feast in his hall ;
He smote on his shield, and each face
　Grew bright as his men heard the call.

His heroes arose, as the waves when the blows
Of the smiting wind fall on their backs as it
　　goes
Shouting defiance along the wide main,
And flinging destruction abroad in the plain.

But above them all, as a lofty rock
Above the billows unmoved by their shock,
The leader of heroes, great Casivel, stood,
And his brow looked like night in his wrath-
　　ful mood.

His spear was like the glittering beam
　Of the setting moon on the ocean's breast,
When the waves are still, or the mountain
　　stream
　Has wooed them, singing, away to rest.

His buckler was like an isle of the sea,
　Which many a storm has smitten in vain ;
Bare and barren, where there may be
　Naught but the marks of the beating main.

He stood, a lofty tower, in whose shade
Securely dwelt the widow and the maid.

Again the Northman called aloud,
His voice was stern, his words were proud, —
Give me two thousand measures of your grains,
A   thousand   of   the   beeves   which   graze   your
        plains,
A hundred of your maids most dutiful,
Full fifty of your wives most beautiful,
And I will peacefully again return
Into my country; else will slay and burn.
Or leave, to make you wretched, still your lives,
Bereft of homes, of children, and of wives.

When these fierce words defiant had been heard,
Each sword flashed fire, every bright spear
        stirred.
But all his heroes wait their chief's command, —
In silent anger frowning near him stand.

Said youthful Carak, by the chieftain loved
For loveliness in many manners proved, —
If thou hast ever loved me, Casivel,
As often I have dearly heard thee tell,
Remain thou here, and let me lead the fight.
Said Casivel: *Go, win thy fame by might.*

Then Carak fair unto the Northman cried, —
Thou son of snows, take back thy words of pride ;
Return in shame into thy mountain lair,
Or I will drive thee hence, and hunt thee there.

The Northman frowned, and up the glen
Came onward with his wrathful men.

So a tall ship upon a wave
  Is borne.   They meet brave Carak's ranks.
Then many a Northman found a grave.
  Like rushing Deva, up its banks,
When Ocean meets it in its track,
Young Carak's ranks are driven back.

He, yielding not, assails his foe.
As two tall oaks, when strong winds blow,
Which on the river's bank have stood
With branches linked, above the flood
In conflict writhe, the foes engage.
But Carak falls before the rage
Of the fell Northman.   Then arose
A cry, as when the storm o'erthrows
Some lofty pine upon the hill :
It rose, then all again was still.

But Casivel, as when the rage
  Of great Taranis rends the rocks.

And lets some torrent from its cage
  By blows of fire and roaring shocks,
With loud outcry moves to the fight,
His golden hair streams rays of light.

Before his course the foes give way:
So yields the night before the day.
The waves, so broken, turn to flee
When the fierce torrent meets the sea.

The great spear poised, one ponderous thrust
Rolls down the Northman in the dust;
His huge shield cleft, his lofty side
Displays a cavern deep and wide.

Their chieftain slain, his men still fly,
But, overtaken, gasping lie.
On them the hawks long feed their brood,
The thirsting wolves long drink their blood.
Their bones are bleached unburied there;
Their ghosts there wander in despair.

A few, submissive, ask for life,
'T is granted, and so ends the strife.

The hero bids them peacefully retire, —
Go to their hills secure, and dread his ire.

Not with linkèd chains,
Not with whip and thong,
Not from captives' pains
Briton shall be strong.
Her firm protection is not prison walls;
It is her sons all ready when she calls.

Such were thy fathers' deeds, Caractacus;
The ghosts of years so whisper them to us.

Before a Cave hollowed among overhanging Rocks in the Bank of a deep Glen.

SEXTUS AND BERNICE. TORSA AND THE THREE PIRATES AT A LITTLE DISTANCE.

SEXTUS.

WHO is this same accursed Kaliphilus?

BERNICE.

That recks not. Speak we of ourselves; we may
Assist each other.

SEXTUS.

Who art thou?

BERNICE.

A woman,
If fickle e'er in love, ne'er in revenge,
Who 'd serve thee, if thou wilt, in turn, do her
A service.

SEXTUS.

How canst thou serve me?

BERNICE.

Were it not
A service, should I free thee?

SEXTUS.

Yea, the greatest.

BERNICE.

This can I do, and furnish thee the means
To find thy way to Gaul.

SEXTUS.

Then I for thee
Will do all that man may.

BERNICE.

Give me a pledge.

SEXTUS.

I 'll pledge thee all I have, — a soldier's honor.

BERNICE.

I must seem bold, for I perceive in thee
That which will not engage in plots ignoble.
And that thou mayest know my plot is fair,
And asketh not what honor may not grant,
I pray thee hear, and think some other tells
Thee of myself. I love Kaliphilus —
Nay, peace, nor ask a woman why she loves,
Nor what, nor chide her for it. He hath made
Me many promises which much concern
My honor.

SEXTUS.

And he keeps them not.

BERNICE.

Nay, listen;
The time is short. There is, upon this isle,
A Roman captive, who should be a queen;
Who, as a queen, rules in all hearts that know
    her.

SEXTUS.

A Roman captive here: a woman too?

BERNICE.

Who, in her turn, hath captured all her captors,
And made them slaves; whose potent loveli-
    ness
Kaliphilus hath mastered, bound in fetters
His will, led all his powers beneath the yoke,
Imprisoned all his promises to me,
And driven me out of my citadel
And home, my trust in him, and his strong
    love,
To wander without succor in a desert.
He says he loves her not; would have me
    think
That he should wed her for some cause of state,
But not for love; and yet I know he loves her.

SEXTUS.

And loves she him?

BERNICE.

She will not tell me so.
But still she doth ; she could not help but love
him.

SEXTUS.

What is thy plan ? How can I help thee in
it ?

BERNICE.

I came to bribe these men to take her hence,
And leave her at the nearest Roman post.
I shudder now to think I would have placed
Her helpless in the power of such fiends.
But thou canst do it safely if thou wilt.

SEXTUS.

How could we leave the isle ?

BERNICE.

A ship awaits
Kaliphilus, who, ere the morning dawn,
Would take her hence to Gaul. That canst
thou have.
And she hath friends who would reward thee ;
for
She is of noble birth.

SEXTUS.

What lineage ?

BERNICE.

The daughter of Herodias —

SEXTUS.

Salome !

BERNICE.

The same.   Know'st thou —

SEXTUS.

I knew her mother well.
She loves Kaliphilus ?

BERNICE.

Ay, as I think.

SEXTUS.

Would wed him ?

BERNICE.

'T is his will ; he 's powerful.

SEXTUS.

I 'll do as thou hast said.   Quick, loose these
      thongs.

BERNICE.

Not while your guards are watchful.   They
      must sleep.
I have a drink, of potent bitterness,
Made by the natives here, and by them loved,
With which they still the hoarse demands of
      care,

Take memory from heavy-limbed fatigue,
Congeal the sluices of o'erflowing sorrow,
Dissolve the spur upon ambition's heel,
Wash out the boundaries 'twixt right and wrong,
And soothe the conscience to untroubled sleep.
This will I bring, and give your guardians
    here;
And in it I will mix a subtle drug,
Which, quickly finding out the seat of life,
So closely shall besiege it that no warden
Shall show himself to answer any summons.
Life's avenues all closed, its springs cut off,
Its scarlet banners from the works withdrawn,
The watchfires all put out, the sentinels
From all the outer posts of sense recalled,
Then, while this power, the counterfeit of
    death,
Holds silent sway, I will return to thee,
And bring with me thy sword and buckler,
    loose,
And let thee freely go to free Salome.

SEXTUS.

She loves Kaliphilus? Thou knowest her well?

BERNICE.

Yea, I may say so.

SEXTUS.

Hast thou heard her tell
Of one, mine own dear friend, — whom once
  she loved, —
Called Sextus?

BERNICE.

He, who's so renowned?

SEXTUS.

Perchance.
A Roman general now — 't was long ago
She loved him.

BERNICE.

She hath never spoke of him.

SEXTUS.

Well — get the liquor quick. But stay; come
  back.
How came she here? .

BERNICE.

I know not, by some wind —
Some pirate chief —

SEXTUS.

Begone, and set me free.

BERNICE.

I will prepare Salome, bring her near
The ship. I think she will not hesitate.
If need be, I can say Kaliphilus
Requested that she go before with thee.
I will corrupt his servant, Theudas, so
He 'll lend thee aid. And if she obstinate,
Should challenge argument of manly force,
Say, wilt thou use it ?

SEXTUS.

By the gods, I will !

BERNICE.

Thou wilt not still refuse to tell thy name ?
I may be powerful to give thee thanks.

SEXTUS.

Nay, do as thou hast said, and I will owe
Such thanks as should be counted out in drops
Of all my blood, each current for a talent.
I pray thee haste and fetch the liquor. Go —
Yet stay. Hath she grown old ? How doth she
      look ?

BERNICE.

A deep and tranquil face reflecting heaven.
I will return anon — and — can I trust thee ?

SEXTUS.

As thou wouldst trust a hare to flee the hounds.
Do but dispatch, and set me free, or else
This fever 'll be before thee in the office.

A Hill-side.

ANTONIUS AND SALOME.

ANTONIUS.

'T IS now the hour when gentle Meditation
Comes fondly to the open arms of Nature.
Now Phœbus lays aside his silver armor,
And, wrapped in scarlet robes, goes to his
    slumber.
So should a blood-stained warrior meet his
    death,
And from it send a glory to illume
The hoary summits of far distant ages,
The shining tops of rolling centuries,
And all the towers and lofty shafts of Fame.

SALOMI

War is a dreadful trade ; and Fame is bad
Who so entices men to such a trade.
So leads the *ignis fatuus* the unwary
To dark perdition in some dreadful moor.

ANTONIUS.

Thou speakest girl-like ; so let women think.

Men are for conflict, else the world would
    stagnate.
The emerald corselets of white plumèd waves,
Which march in serried columns to the shore,
Are stained by the last flight of rushing rays
From Phoebus' quiver —

SALOME.

        Yet they stagger on —

ANTONIUS.

Like ranks of wounded demi-gods, to die
In the forefront far up the breachèd shore.
Around me in my final hour I 'd fold
A bloody mantle, and in growing storms,
Before perturbèd ranks of falling foes,
Let my enthralled and stormy soul break forth —
What men are they who move upon the beach
Where foot to foot the sea and land contend
For empire?

SALOME.

      They are some body of the natives
Preparing for some warlike expedition.

ANTONIUS.

Methinks they seem to place a guard along
The shore.

SALOME.

Nay, that is not their wont. But say,
My father —

ANTONIUS.

What is it, my girl? Sit here
Upon my knee, as when thou wert a child.

SALOME.

Nay, let me sit by thee.

ANTONIUS.

Fie! baby, fie!
Why, thou didst sit upon thy father's knee
When last I saw thee. Ah! how thou didst
    prattle,
And pull thy mother's hair.

SALOME.

My mother!

ANTONIUS.

Ay,
And try to sing old songs thy nurse had taught
    thee.
Ah! kiss me, child. It seems but yesterday.
And yet thou art grown so, — thou art little
    like
My baby then. It seems to me as if
My joy at finding thee had made my mind

A little weak, Salome. I am old,
A little over-fond, and childish — eh ?

SALOME.

Nay, father.   When joy melts the wintry bands
Which check the easy flowing of our thoughts,
They overrun and take strange currents oft, —
Oft flow in many diverse, babbling streams.
When didst thou learn of my poor mother's
    death ?

ANTONIUS.

Why, girl, I saw her die.

SALOME.

                              Thou didst !

ANTONIUS.

                                        I did.

SALOME.

And thou wert at Jerusalem that night?

ANTONIUS.

Ay, coming home to Rome; was bidden too
By Herod to his feast, but would not go —

SALOME.

Oh, speak not of that feast ! Oh, spare me
    that !

ANTONIUS.

Thou art right, girl, — for a night so black
        should be
By its own horrid blackness deep engulfed,
And no words e'er evoke its frightful ghost.

SALOME.

Thou knowest not what cause I have to dread
And shudder at the memory of that night.
Sometime I will unload my burdened heart
Into thy willing ear.

ANTONIUS.

                    Whene'er thou wilt.
Who march with wild outcry of threatening war
Across the isle, from its remotest end ?

SALOME.

They are Britons, just now landed from the
        shore
Of the great island.

ANTONIUS.

                    What betokens this
Harsh sound of preparation ?

SALOME.

                    'T is some feud

Perchance, broke forth between the neighbor-
    ing tribes,
For civil wars and contests are their sport.
My father, I would ask — I wish to know —

ANTONIUS.

Well, daughter, what wouldst ask? what wish
    to know?

SALOME.

Didst thou e'er see — or hast thou ever heard
Of one, a youthful officer — a Roman —
Called Sextus?

ANTONIUS.

       Did I know him? Ah, my child,
E'en as a son. I know thy story, love.
He told me all.

SALOME.

      Where is he now, my father?

ANTONIUS.

Now, that I will not tell; thou 'lt think of him
And so forget this fond, old, jealous father.

SALOME.

Ah, I could ne'er do that. Oh, tell me.

ANTONIUS.

                          Nay,
Not till I hear thee tell me of thyself.

SALOME.

But, is he well? I pray thee, tell me this.

ANTONIUS.

Kiss me, my child.

SALOME.

Not till thou answer me.

ANTONIUS.

Yea, he is well; at least he was —

SALOME.

He was!

But when?

ANTONIUS.

When last I spoke with him.

SALOME.

O fie!

ANTONIUS.

Thou hast not asked me wherefore I am here.

SALOME.

Because I thought my father would make known
All of himself he wished his child to know.

ANTONIUS.

Right, girl. Well, shall I tell thee?

SALOME.

Pray thee do.

ANTONIUS.

Three times the morn hath drawn the veiling
    night
From Earth's fair face, and wakened her with
    kisses
Since, with the general Plautius, we embarked
From hither coast of Gaul, and gave ourselves
To guidance of soft breezes from the south,
Which falsely promised us fair passage to
The southern coast of Briton, with our army.
It was our duty there again to take
Fresh pledges of allegiance, and enlarge
The bounds of the Republic, moved thereto
By Claudius, the emperor's, commands.
But, ere we reached the shining British cliffs,
An adverse wind rushed from its icy cave, —
Beyond where Thule groans beneath the weight
Of snows piled ceaselessly by Winter's hand, —
Sprang on our vessels, tore our sails away,
Snatched all our oars, or brake them in our grasp,
And, roaring, drove us from our wished-for
    course.
The seas grew angry, ope'd a hundred mouths,
And held us, writhing, in their foaming jaws :
Then, mocking, spat us forth, again to mouth us.
While thus we were their sport, the south-west
    wind

Came foaming on us with an angry shriek.
Then, 'twixt the winds and the voracious seas,
A contest rose which made the heavens hide
Their faces, each contending for the prey,
Till we were torn in pieces, ships all broke,
And after swallowed by the snarling seas.
Our company all sank into their throats,
But me, who, senseless on the beach, was found
By this Kaliphilus, who used me well,
Till, some few hours gone, when he saw fit
To play the traitor, and imprison me.

SALOME.

Imprison thee !

ANTONIUS.

Yea, where thy Thona found me.

SALOME.

But wherefore ?

ANTONIUS.

· Then I could not tell; yet now
I know it was to keep me from thy view.
Now let me know of thee.   How cam'st thou
      here,
And wherefore ?   Do I look as thou hadst
      thought
Thy father should?

SALOME.

The same in nobleness —

ANTONIUS.

But older, thou wouldst say; more scarred,—
    is 't not ?
Yet thou wilt love me, girl ; thou shalt not help
But love me ; I shall spoil thee so.   Eh, bird ?
Say thou wilt love me ; promise me, or else
I 'll squeeze this little hand to half its size,
And then 't will be so small thou canst not
    find it.

SALOME.

I love thee now — but tell me more of Sextus.
He is alive — I long had thought — or feared —

ANTONIUS.

I shall be jealous ! Tell me now thy story.
Our Sextus told me why from him thou fledest,
And hid thyself from the long search of love.
So, go thou on from there.

SALOME.

            I will, but briefly.
I dared not love, nor grieve, nor hope, nor wish ;
I only dared despair, and hid beneath
The ragged wings of wretchedness ; and there
With terror I remained, while darker grew
The dreadful darkness round my shrinking soul.
On me, thus darkened, shone life-giving light —
A hand divine uplifted me thus fallen.

I lived again, as risen from the dead,
And labored to forget all I had loved
In that wrong former life ; but chiefly Sextus,
For so his love was wrought into my love
That our affections were but warp and woof
Of a most bright and perfect web of life.
I gave myself to charity, and lived
With the disciples at Jerusalem.
Thou knowest already that I am a Christian,
And art not angry ?

ANTONIUS.

    Child, may I not err ?
All good ways lead unto Elysium.

SALOME.

Then came the persecution. In the night
I heard a voice which bade me straight go forth.
But whither could I go nor chance to meet
The imploring eyes of him so much beloved?
How see, and still resist his prayers and tears ?
While doubting thus again I heard the voice, —
I came not to destroy, but to fulfill.
I came not to uproot, but to engraft.
Dwarf not thyself by blighting any power,
Nor bury any talent in the earth ;
Nor mutilate the fair proportions of
Thy soul, as it was formed by the Creator.

Inaction is no service; I demand
Full action of all faculties, controlled
By love for Me, so that all things be done
But for My Father's glory. All His works,
And every part of all, were by Him made.
The self-denial, which I ask, is not
Destruction, but subordination; not
Eradication, but conformity.
Next after love for Me, My gospel asks
Love for a spouse, for children, parents, friends,
And that true love for Me through love for them
Be shown. Easy My yoke; My burden light.
Thus freed from zealous ignorance, no more
A captive blind, and chained, and harshly
 driven
By self-denials thwarting laws of God, .
In nature written, sought I to atone
For sin, and by no suffering self-imposed.
And now I felt how I had wronged my Sextus,
By scourging him that I might lash myself;
How easy in the pride of humbleness
To be the minions of most unjust pride;
And, with professèd holy zeal, inflict
Such wrongs as demons only should invent.
Perceived how honestly man can be wrong,
And learned distrust of self; learned charity.
I wished to stay the wrong which I had caused
To my beloved Sextus and myself.

ANTONIUS.

Why didst thou not seek Sextus, let him
  know —

SALOME.

I went to Rome; too late, for there I heard
That Sextus with his forces was in Spain.
There patient duty, and impatient love
Impelled me. Soon a goodly company
Was sent to him; together I set sail,
With letters of safe-conduct from the court.
But when we came about the southern cape,
And would cast anchor in the northern bay,
A force of British pirates took our ship,
And captives brought as hither. All but me
Were burnt in sacrifice to druid gods.

ANTONIUS.

And why wert thou not sacrificed with them?

SALOME.

Kaliphilus had ta'en me from my captors
And would not give me up.

ANTONIUS.
                    The gods reward him.

SALOME.

Yet was I in great danger; for the King,

14

Caractacus, beheld me, and at once
Would take me from Kaliphilus, to be
His own familiar slave.   Kaliphilus
Opposed him.   Then the King, in anger,
        swore
Kaliphilus should die.   But when he saw
That they could not confine him ; that no force
Of open war, or subtlety could kill,
They feared him and desisted ; and thence-
        forth
I was as one protected by their gods.
The druid chief, an old man venerable,
Of purest life, the almoner and steward
Of fair Benevolence, took pity on me
And led me to his home, to his dear daughter,
To be her near companion.   It was she
Who brought thee to me —

ANTONIUS.

                    On that distant shore,
Where fast upon the land's white breast the
        waves,
Like children wearied with their play, all
        come
To lay their heads and nestle there to rest,
What company is that, who, clad in robes
Of white and blue, are gathering trees in piles,
And look like flocks of sea-birds building nests ?

SALOME.

They are British priests.

ANTONIUS.

What mean those woody heaps?

SALOME.

The preparation for some festival.
But tell me now of Sextus; pain me not
By longer silence. Why that troubled look?
Thou said'st that he was well. Oh, tell me,
father.

ANTONIUS.

I said that he was well when last we talked —

SALOME.

Thou turn'st away thy face. What mean those
tears?
Hath aught befallen him? Oh, lives he still?

ANTONIUS.

My child, since last I pressed his hand I 've
heard
That a most potent illness preyed on him —

SALOME.

Oh, let 's go to him. Where is he? Let 's go.

ANTONIUS.

Nay, daughter, 't were too far for thy poor
    strength.

SALOME.

But I am very strong. Oh, let us go.
O father, let me see him ere he die.

ANTONIUS.

I fear, my love, he be already dead.

SALOME.

Say not so ; — no, let 's go to him. Alas !
We 're captives, and he knows it not ! If free —

ANTONIUS.

We could not see him. He will surely die.
Come nearer to me, girl, and lean thy head
On my old breast. Nay, grieve not so, my
    child.

SALOME.

I know all now — I know that he is dead.

ANTONIUS.

Yea, daughter ; he is in Elysium.

SALOME.

When was it ? Did he speak of me ?

ANTONIUS.

Alas !
I was not by him.

SALOME.

Did he love me still ?

ANTONIUS.

Yea, while he lived; and only thee.

SALOME.

Oh, say,
Had he forgiven me ?

—

ANTONIUS.

He never thought
He had aught to forgive.

SALOME.

Where did he die ?

ANTONIUS.

Raise now thy head, and look upon the sea.
Where yonder rock, like some huge monster, lifts
Its back above the waves, his ship went down.

SALOME.

Alas, so near !

ANTONIUS.

It was but yesterday,
In the great storm, when all our fleet was
    wrecked.
Ah me! I know not how to comfort thee.
Weep, weep and moan; he was worth all thy
    tears.

SALOME.

The bitterness of my captivity
Is passed. Though free as clouds, I could not
    find him,
Nor hear him speak the blessed words of pardon.
Ah me! alas, his voice shall speak no more,
That used to woo me like the dove's complaint!

ANTONIUS.

But when he gave command in battle it was
Like Jove's, while marshaling the distant worlds,
When storms in whirling darkness whelm the
    heavens.

SALOME.

He spoke to me of peace, and on his brow
The smiling sunshine played.

ANTONIUS.

But, when he frowned,
The camp was hushed and suddenly grew dark.

SALOME.

That he should be so near me but to perish,
Unknowing both ! O Heavenly Father, help me,
Let me not be rebellious !

ANTONIUS.

Thou, ere long,
Shalt wander with him in the Elysian Fields.
This life seems long, it is so wearisome,
But yet 't is short; wait but a little while.

SALOME.

Our souls were as two echoes, which repeat
Each other; and of their sweet song the rise,
The burden, and the cadence were but turns,
And varied melodies on themes of love,
Forever seeking for some new-made strain
To say, with deeper meaning, how we loved.

ANTONIUS.

His dear love never waned : we sought thee still
When Hope had grown all weary, and Despair,
With random steps, served us alone as guide.
'T is true, while marching hitherward through
      Gaul,
A soldier, who had long a captive been
Among the German tribes, sought Sextus out,
And gave a tablet travel-stained and worn,

Which bore a message from thee ; but 't was
    old,
And could not tell nor when nor where 't was
    writ.

SALOME.

What was it, pray ? I have so many sent.

ANTONIUS.

I well remember it ; 't is transcribed here —
O Sextus, I am coming to thee, thine.
Forgive me all thy wrongs, and still be mine.
While we both live, united or apart,
Thou hast alone, and wholly hast, my heart.

SALOME.

This knowledge is some comfort ; kept he it ?
What did he do ?

ANTONIUS.

          He wore it on his heart,
Embalmed with kisses and bepearled with
    tears.
But tell me more of your young loves ; 't will
    soothe
And comfort thee, my child : it comforts me.

SALOME.

This is the hour when we by mutual compact

Each on the other thought, and so kept tryst,
By the assurèd meeting of our spirits,
According to the lover's powerful faith.
And where yon star, which now begins to
     station
Upon the golden ramparts of the west
Its glittering ranks of spearmen, takes its stand,
Was, for our eyes, the appointed place of meet-
     ing.
Oft have I watched it till its fires were
     quenched
By the flood tide of morning rolling westward,
And tried to pierce its solid, silver portals
Into its treasure-house, from mortals hidden,
To read there if he lived; still at this hour
Were thinking but of me; and still were gaz-
     ing,
As I, upon that star, with look more ardent
Than is its own, as he would fascinate it
From its high sphere, and know from it the
     tidings
Of me; and from its keep take out the message
Of love, which, night by night, mine eyes have
     placed there.

ANTONIUS.

This feeding sorrow on remembrance may
But too much strengthen sorrow till it hold

The sole dominion where joy too should reign
With equal sceptre. Let us not forget
That, in this grief, we are not all unhappy.
For we have found each other; and ere long
We shall find means to quit this prisonment.
The Emperor will surely send again
An army to complete this conquest; then,
Set free, we 'll go to Rome, and there, as swal-
          lows
Come back to nests deserted in old gables,
When scowling winter yields to smiling spring,
We 'll flit away a bright and joyous summer.
For, since I have thee, I am young again ;
And we shall have so much to tell each other,
The very birds themselves shall stop and listen
To our more constant chirping.   Now good
          e'en.
Upon yon amber mountain in the East
The Evening 'gins to place its sentinels,
Whose burnished shields shall mark their sleep-
          less posts
Throughout the night.   Go thou within awhile.
I will approach to see what make these Britons.

SALOME.

Nay, come with me ; thou art a stranger here.
If any thing befall thee —

ANTONIUS.

Timid dear!
Fear nothing, girl; I will be cautious — go.

SALOME.

And thou wilt soon come back?

ANTONIUS.

Ay, soon, my child.
By naught but thee can I be now beguiled.

[*Exit* SALOME.

Now will I know what mean these British
    thieves,
Who for an hour have lurked about the wood,
Thinking themselves unseen. Whate'er they be,
I am no soldier if they purpose good
To me or mine — how precious is that mine!
Till now unknown by me. Kaliphilus
Is but a traitor. I would sooner trust
These savages. Mercurius be my guide.
Unsafe I go; but more unsafe abide.

BERNICE AND SEXTUS.

BERNICE.

WITHIN that thicket thou wilt find thine arms.
There must thou hide thyself. I 've tried in
vain
To win his servant, Theudas, to our plot;
He threatened to report it to his master,
But that I fear not. Now the ship is ready;
And, with my help, once here she must aboard.
The wind is fair, and — canst thou find thy way
To Gaul?

SEXTUS.

Ay, never fear.

BERNICE.

Or where thou wilt;
I care not whither, so it be from here.

SEXTUS.

But will she come? The night already marks
The hour when trembling Weariness woos
Slumber,

Who, smiling, opes her arms, and softly draws
His drooping head upon her dream-veiled bosom,
And gentle-fingered Dian gilds their rest.

BERNICE.

Yea, she will come. I charged her dear-loved
    friend,
The maiden Thona, who knows well this spot,
To tell her that a shipwrecked soldier here
Demanded instant aid; with such enticement
She 'll surely come. She never yet refused
Such kindly offices by night or day,
In sun's heat, or in tempest.

SEXTUS.

                  If she bring
Kaliphilus with her —

BERNICE.

              Oh, fear it not;
She cannot; he prepares for his departure.

SEXTUS.

Yet, if she love him —

BERNICE.

            If! I know it now.
Within this half hour, as I hither came,

I skirted by the wood upon the hill,
That none might see me. There beheld I her
With him in close and loving converse, such
As Love delights in when the blushing Eve
Is won by the on-coming, eager Night.

SEXTUS.

But art thou sure 't was he ?

BERNICE.

                'T is true the veil
Of evening fell somewhat upon them both.
Yet saw I well it was his manly form ;
And, at this hour, no man, but him, is here.

SEXTUS.

O love !   'T is past belief !

BERNICE.

              'T is strange, indeed.
I saw his arm bent lovingly about her,
Her head was resting happy on his breast.
I saw them kiss —

SEXTUS.

O Furies !

BERNICE.

Thou art moved.

SEXTUS.

I so detest him I would have none love him.
Did'st thou hear aught?

BERNICE.

I could not, till he rose
To leave her for a while, and then she said
In plaintive accents, as of one who'd wept,
In tones of love, which make such partings seem
O'erfull of woe : *And thou wilt soon come back?*

SEXTUS.

And what said he?

BERNICE.

I could not stay to hear,
Lest I should be discovered, and delay
Make our fair plot miscarry. Some one comes.

SEXTUS.

I'll leave her here. I will not take her hence.

BERNICE.

But thou art pledged.

SEXTUS.

Gods! — I'll redeem my pledge.

Enter THONA.

THONA.

Bernice, O Bernice, help! O help!

BERNICE.

What is it?

THONA.

Oh, they 've taken away Salome.

SEXTUS.

Who! What!

THONA.

They 've taken away Salome.

BERNICE.

Who?

THONA.

The priests. Oh, where 's Kaliphilus?

SEXTUS.

The priests!

THONA.

They 've taken her away. Alas, alas!

SEXTUS.

When did they take her? Whither? Why?

THONA.

Ah, me!
They 'll sacrifice her. Where 's Kaliphilus?
He 'd save her.

BERNICE.

Stay thy weeping, let us know,
In order, what has happened.

THONA.

Oh, she's gone!
I had just told her that a soldier here
Her aid demanded; we were setting forth,
When, suddenly, a priest and band of warriors
As 't were, sprang from the ground and seized
her.

SEXTUS.

Fiends!

THONA.

They stopped her mouth —

SEXTUS.

O villains.

THONA.

Bound her fast,
And quickly bore her thence.

SEXTUS.

But whither?

THONA.

Ah!
I know not. Save, O save her, sir.

15

SEXTUS.

I will.

THONA.

Alas! Thou canst not.   Oh, I know too well —

SEXTUS.

But we must find her.   Come, point out the
way.
I 'll save her, or with men no longer stay.

A Sacred Grove near the Sea-shore.

CARACTACUS, ALPINDARGO, RANMOR, KALIPHILUS, ULLIN, ORLA, THEUDAS, SALOME, DRUIDS, BARDS, AND WARRIORS.

DRUIDS.

TERRIBLE are the gods when they rise in their
    anger.
Then the heavens sink ; they roll blackly to-
    gether ;
Then the forests bow, and rend off their dark
    garments ;
Then in mists earth hides her tear-covered
    visage ;
Then the isles faint and lie hid under waters ;
Then the dark sea grows pale while it trembles.

ARCH DRUIDS.

Shall man
Of feeble hand,
Who cannot stay the waves,
Nor call the islands from the deep,
Nor lift the veil from off the earth's sad face,
Nor raise the bent and sobbing forests,
Nor still the rolling heavens,
Withstand the gods
Alone ?

DRUIDS.

Come, now, let us, too, bow,
Let us appease their wrath,
Let us propitiate their favor.
Then we, victorious,
Shall teach insulting foes
How vainly they defy our gods.

ARCH DRUIDS.

The altar is prepared ; come near,
  And, ere the sacrifice is made,
Call, so that all the gods may hear
  And lend us their resistless aid.

DRUIDS.

Be thanked, ye gods, and honored.
When ye came riding forth on fire-breathing
      clouds
We all stood up to praise ye.
When, with tornadoes in your hands
Ye swept the stranger's vessels from the sea,
We shouted to your glory, and our bards sang
      hymns.
In your great wrath we trusted and rejoiced.
Now let our thanks come to you,
Like sweetest song of bards when feasts are
      spread.
Be thanked, ye gods, and honored.

Waken! O gods, awake!
Come from the cloudy chase,
Rise from the feast of shells.

DRUIDS.

Accept our sacrifice,
And help us.

ALPINDARGO.

Jow, who keepest the winds
In thy blue dwelling nailed with stars,
Smite our foes with blasts.

DRUIDS.

Accept our sacrifice,
And help us.

ALPINDARGO.

Bel, thou father of days,
Come on thy car of fire,
Burn our foes before us.

DRUIDS.

Accept our sacrifice,
And help us.

ALPINDARGO.

Hesus, with hands dripping blood,
Come with the wailing of storms,
Tear in pieces our foes.

DRUIDS.

Accept our sacrifice,
And help us.

ALPINDARGO.

Thou, Taranis, who ridest
Trampling the wreck of the heavens,
Shake our foes with thy voice.

DRUIDS.

Accept our sacrifice,
And help us.

ALPINDARGO.

Thou, Teutates, who knowest
Ways to beguile and seduce,
Lead our foes from their course.

DRUIDS.

Accept our sacrifice,
And help us.

ARCH DRUIDS.

Our victim is a chosen one,
Most comely; of the hated race
Of our great enemies — a maiden.
She should be pleasing to ye gods.
She is the best we have,
So take her dearly from us.

ALPINDARGO.

Oh, she is dear to me as mine own blood,
More dear to me than life.   Hear me, ye gods:
Oh, let this worthy sacrifice prevail
To save this people, and preserve these rites.
My child, it is not man — the gods demand thee.

SALOME.

God, the Lord Omnipotent, reigneth:
His justice cannot err.   His will be done.

CARACTACUS.

I will have thine, if e'er I change religions:

ULLIN.

Hear me, O Druids.   Priests, abstain awhile.
Ye know that, in the measure of the gods,
Man equals man ; the proudest head, for them,
Hath not a greater price than lowliest
When placed upon their altar.   What most dear
To suppliants is dearest unto them.
As in the suppliant's estimation named
They value it.   Ah! were it otherwise,
Did they regard the victim's worth alone,
As balanced in the human scale of worth,
Or their calm eyes rejoice in woman's beauty
The captive standing at the altar here
Should be to them the dearest sacrifice.

But we shall presently be in great need.
The stranger's ships shall smite again our shore,
And Briton's heroes vainly fall, unless
The gods shall help us. Let us then prevail
By offering something dearer to ourselves
Than this poor captive. Since naught is more
    dear
Unto ourselves than our own selves, behold!
I claim the right to immolate myself.

ALL.

Thou!

ALPINDARGO.

O my son! my son!

SALOME.

Nay, Ullin, nay —

ULLIN.

I will not say that none is here more dear
Than I; nor boast how dearly I am held;
Yet were ungrateful — nay, I were most false,
If, with immodest show of modesty,
I should deny your truth, and name myself
Unloved. Not few, nor poor your proofs of
    love,
As due to your loved chieftain's only son.
And thou, O chief, my father, grudge me not

If I devote myself to save this people.
Ye heard his cry of agony; ye see
His silent tears; ye know his strength of heart.
Judge then, O Druids, if I be not dear,
And let me win immortal fame this night,
While, as a hero, with my life I save
That of my country and of those I love.

SALOME.

Thou art most generous, noble Ullin; yet
Bethink thee of the precepts thou hast heard,
And so do not this wrong to thee and thine.

ULLIN.

Now, let this captive maiden go in peace,
And grant my prayer; it is an ancient right.
Advance, and do on me your office, priests.

RANMOR.

There is an ancient law, long since forgot,
While lying hidden in old druid lore,
Unneeded and unused. This law declares
The chosen victim shall be of the race
Of our most imminent foes; and it forbids
Self-immolation at this holy feast,
Or victim chosen from another race.
The holy Alpindargo knows the law.

ALPINDARGO.

Most true — I had forgot — these heavy years —
My son, it must not be.

ULLIN.

O cruel priest.

RANMOR.

But if, O pious youth, thou needs must die
To serve thy country, thou shalt have occasion:
Leave but thy harp, and lift the spear in battle;
There immolate thyself, if so thou wilt.

KALIPHILUS.

O Druids, Bards, and Warriors, let me speak.

ALL.

The great magician! Listen.

ALPINDARGO.

We attend.

KALIPHILUS.

Well hath wise Ranmor counseled you. This
law
Should now prevail; and this brave youth
should live.

RANMOR.

Ye hear, ye hear: he speaketh like a god!

ULLIN.

But thou did'st tell me —

KALIPHILUS.

True ; I told thee so.
If one who loved her truly could be found,
And he would give himself to die for her
That she should live.

ULLIN.

Here I so give myself.

KALIPHILUS.

And she shall live. For know the potency
Of offerings, fond youth, is in the intent,
Not in the acceptance ; and in thine intent
Thou art offered. Thou shalt live. Hear, holy
       men,
If I produce a captive warrior,
One great in power, as in name ; whose sword
Shall else, a treacherous bale-fire, lead to wreck
A fleet of British souls now sailing fair
On life's night-bounded sea ; a Roman too,
Will ye this maiden captive grant me freely ?

RANMOR.

It shall not be —

ALPINDARGO.

He speaketh like a god!
It shall be so; ay, vengeful priest, it shall.

DRUIDS.

Good.　Let it be so.　Lead thy warrior hither.

KALIPHILUS.

Now, Theudas, bid them bring their prisoner.

[*Exit* THEUDAS.

KALIPHILUS.

So all goes well; and by this subtle strife
I 'll lose a rival and will gain a wife.

Enter THEUDAS *with armed men, leading in* ANTONIUS *bound.*

SALOME.

My father!

KALIPHILUS.

Yea, my fair one; none but he.

ANTONIUS.

What, daughter! here in chains! What meaneth
this?

SALOME.

Kaliphilus, how couldst thou so betray!

KALIPHILUS.

To win thee.

ANTONIUS.

Perjured host, false prophet, knave,
Thou traitor; was it not enough for thee
To so beguile the father.

KALIPHILUS.

Ha, ha, ha!

SALOME.

Kaliphilus, O save him. Save my father!

ANTONIUS.

What would they with thee here, my child?

SALOME.

Behold
The altar.

ANTONIUS.

No! It cannot be! Forbid,
Ye mighty gods. Break, fetters, break, or else
The opposeless rage in me will burst its bounds,
And I a helpless ruin topple down.
They shall not do it.

SALOME.

Thou, alas! art here
To take my place.

ANTONIUS.

Ay, that I will, my girl.
Since these bloodthirsty villains must taste blood,
Let mine suffice. The flood throbs in thy veins ;
My currents ebb e'en at their fountain head.

SALOME.

O Heavenly Father, help —

KALIPHILUS.

He cannot do it.
I, I alone, can save thy father.

SALOME.

Thou !
And wilt not ? O Kaliphilus, have pity.
See his gray hairs. O save him !

ANTONIUS.

Hush ! my child.
If one of us must die 't is I. Alas !
But e'en this morn and death had met me
glad
For the encounter : I was childless then.
This new, too late found happiness, is yet
A smiling infant, still too young to know
How sweet its own existence. Must I leave
thee ?

ALPINDARGO.

Magician, lo! our rites are all delayed.

KALIPHILUS.

Go, Theudas, to the glen where shadows sleep
The livelong day; thou 'lt find in savage guard
A Roman; bring him hither bound. But keep
Him from our sight until I bid him here.

- [*Exit* THEUDAS.

ANTONIUS.

To let thee die were kindness. Leave thee here
With this vile knave! — Gods, have ye yet in
    store
Pains bitterer; more cruel mockeries?
O Fates implacable, not yet appeased?
But ye are stronger than a poor old man,
Who still would struggle underneath the weight
Of your great curses, so to save his child,
And challenge still your great resistless wills
To heap mount upon mount, until at length
Beneath great Alpine ranges he be crushed —
As I am now — I can resist no more.

ALPINDARGO.

Kaliphilus, take thou the maiden hence;
She may not see what follows: take her hence.

[SALOME *is unbound and set free.*

SALOME.

Nay, set my father free. Kaliphilus,
Wilt thou do naught for me? and thou hast
    said —

KALIPHILUS.

What have I said? Speak out.

SALOME.

O save him! save him!

[*Priests approach and lay hands on* ANTONIUS.

ANTONIUS.

Farewell, my child. Come here, embrace me
    once —
The good gods help thee, daughter. Fare thee
    well.

KALIPHILUS.

Salome, thou art mine. I 've ransomed thee,
I 've bought thee, paid for thee the old man
    there.
Yet, though thou art mine own, my captive
    slave,
I still would treat thee as my ruling queen,
And hear thy full consent to be mine own.

SALOME.

It cannot be.

ANTONIUS, *looking back as he is led toward the altar.*

Right, girl; no — never, never.

KALIPHILUS.

Then be thy father's murderer, if thou wilt,
Ay, and my wife unwedded. Thou art mine.

SALOME.

O chief, good Alpindargo, help me now.
This is my father; I his daughter am.
O save him ; send him hence. O slay him not ;
A father should not die to save his child.
'T is fit the child should save the father's life.
Do as thou had'st determined: let me die.
Thou had'st a father ; think thou hast him still.
As thou would'st save him so let me save mine.
O Alpindargo, O good priest, O help me !

ALPINDARGO.

Alas ! my child, who can direct the gods,
Or change their stern decrees? I cannot help
    thee.

KALIPHILUS.

But I can help thee — stern decrees of gods !
The gods prefer a warrior to a girl,
A youthful warrior to one weak with age.
A youthful warrior can I yet provide,
And save Salome, and her father too,
If she will here consent to be my wife.

16

ALPINDARGO.

And canst thou hesitate, my child ?

SALOME.

                                   Alas !
O Heaven, help me !   Save him — I am thine.

KALIPHILUS.

Give me thy hand, then.   Come into my arms.

Enter SEXTUS, *followed by* BERNICE *and* THONA; *they stand unseen.* SALOME *gives her hand to* KALIPHILUS, *who draws her into his arms.*

KALIPHILUS.

Rest here upon my breast.   Say thou art mine.

SALOME.

Yea, I am thine —

BERNICE *to* SEXTUS.

                         I told thee so.

SEXTUS, *coming forward.*

                                 O gods !
So thou art his ?   Thine own words so declare ?

SALOME.

Ah ! Sextus !

KALIPHILUS.

      In good time.   Arrest him there.
Confess my power; I said I would produce him.

SEXTUS.

I would believe no other — wherefore thee ?
But 't is a vicious habit I have learned.
O thou multiplicate and compound lie,
Thou living falsehood, thou duplicity,
Quintessence of all guile ; thou clinging lie,
Thou lie Briarean, each separate hand
Of all thy hundred is a complex lie,
The pressure of each separate finger lies,
Thy friend-like grasp a volume is of lies,
Thou art thyself a library of lies —

SALOME.

O spare me, Sextus.

SEXTUS.

      Here 's thy written pledge :
O Sextus, I am coming to thee, thine.
Forgive me all thy wrongs, and still be mine.
While we both live, united or apart,
Thou hast alone, and wholly hast, my heart.

SALOME.

O Sextus, it was true, — is true, is true.

SEXTUS.

What! spring they still fresh hatched from thee ?
    Now ? here ?
Thou art a wilderness wherein they dwell,
In wild bloom rank, and fragrant beauty rich.
They ooze from every pore, creep from thine
    eyes,
Coil in thy throat, glide from thine opening lips,
And wriggle in the smile about thy mouth.

SALOME.

Ah me ! alas ! O hear me, Sextus — hear me.

SEXTUS.

Yet veil'st thou them with such a dear outside
Thou art taken by thy lovers all for truth ;
Yet art to each of them a different shape
By thyself multiplied. Thine angel-form,
Oh, it would win with its sweet looks of sooth
Great Jove to give Olympus to thy care,
And be a humble suitor at thy court.
The fiends of hell shrink from thee, envious,
And curse thee that thou so excell'st their art :
Thou Hydra-headed lie, I curse thee — curse
    thee.

KALIPHILUS.

Arrest him there. What, ho !

SEXTUS.

Nay, stand ye back,
For madness will have scope, and I am mad.
Stand back! here dangers spring.   Give me
　　this form.

[*Snatches* SALOME, *who has fainted, from* KALIPHILUS.

Dead? dead? No breath; no pressure in thy
　　hand?
All still? The light gone out in these sweet orbs?
Then is the world all dark, earth paralyzed,
The breezes all grown stiff, the rigid air
Is mute, its starry eyes are fixed with grief.
No word, my love, my child? No more fare-
　　wells?
My burning kiss cannot relight these lamps?
Apollo, bring back day unto the world.
Ah, Sextus, it is time for thee to go,
The damps of night shall give thee chills and
　　woe!

KALIPHILUS.

Now would he gladly die while he believes
She loves him not; so let him live until,
From her own lips, he know himself beloved,
Then shall he taste the bitterness of death.

[ANTONIUS *breaking away from the priests, by whom he
has been surrounded and concealed.*

Away! give place.   I tell ye I will see

Who so usurps the accents of my Sextus, —
Whose grief so sounds in unison with mine —

SEXTUS.

Antonius! come back to chide me —

ANTONIUS.

Sextus!

SEXTUS. .

Art thou alive? then stand thou farther off,
Wouldest thou not die; for here 's a sight to blast
Thy vision, burn, e'en at its fount, thy blood,
And dry up all the sources of thy life?
Thy daughter lies here dead. 'T was I who
killed her.

ANTONIUS.

'T is better thus. She would have lived the wife
Of this black devil, who 'd make her his by force.
The virtue of old Rome still lives in thee.
I, like Virginius, had done the deed,
But that these coward villains held me bound.
We now have nothing more to do, but die
As Romans. She was dear — but — be a man.

SEXTUS.

Now look you, see that brow, how fair, — that
mouth;

Yet falsehood played upon those archèd lips
As poisoned air upon a lute's soft strings,
And made the sweetest music. Woe to him
Who breathed those sounds enchanting— woe
    to me!

ANTONIUS.

He 's mad.

SEXTUS.

    Yet one last kiss, O sweetly false.

SALOME.

O Sextus.

SEXTUS.

    Hush! she speaks. She lives! she lives!

SALOME.

O Sextus, Sextus, art thou come at last?

SEXTUS.

Would to the gods I were not come, to find
Thee false, myself deceived — deceived by thee.
Had the great heavens above me disappeared;
At glaring mid-day, from its middle course,
The sun fell hissing in the ocean's midst,
Set it aflame, and burned it to dry land;
The wild hills run away, with panic stricken;
The mountains fled into the darksome north;
Had all the rivers to their sources rushed,

And crept back shuddering to the womb of
      Earth,
I could have witnessed it unscathed, and said,
This, this is possible.   But thou — by thee —
By thee deceived, betrayed, and all my faith,
My universe of love, grown great and strong,
Thus overwhelmed — it cannot be — what is?
My senses play me false, my reason cries
Loud falsehoods, and my memory is a liar.
I'm false unto myself, and every part
Betrays the other.   Whither shall I go
For truth? Where find a real world? Whom
      trust.?
Now let the great orbs melt away in mists,
And every thing be night; the darkling earth
Be changed, and I in it dissolve and cease. —
Gods! but there is no earth, nor sky, nor orbs.
I'm from a troublous dream unduly waked,
To find myself unreal — a dreaming dream.
Thy truth unreal, the realest of all things.
Then all things are unreal, and I but hope
To awaken to unreal unconsciousness.

ANTONIUS.

Nay, Sextus, wrong her not; she loved but thee.

SALOME.

Oh, always, Sextus.

SEXTUS.

Hold, hold, mock me not.
I heard her pledge herself to him.

SALOME.

Alas!

ANTONIUS.

It was to save my life. She thought thee dead.
I told her so.

SALOME.

Oh, I have loved but thee. —
Have sought thee. O forgive me — can'st thou,
Sextus,
All this long misery? I thought to do
But what was right —

SEXTUS.

O changing dream, avaunt!
How many phantoms take their place in thee,
And sway me to their will. Nay, pardon me
My hot fierce words, my curses, born of love
Struck by the rasping flint of jealousy.
I have been played upon, deceived, alas!
The time sufficeth not to tell thee how —

SALOME.

I knew thou wert abused. 'T is well at last.

ANTONIUS.

Now softly, Sextus. It is plain we die.
We 're in the power of these wild demons here.
Salome must go with us ; else she lives
The slave of this accursed Kaliphilus.
Lend me thy sword.

> *Takes the sword, and is about to stab* SALOME, *when he is prevented and disarmed by* KALIPHILUS.

KALIPHILUS.

Ha, ha, old man ! too late.
Why stand ye gazing, priests ? Secure your victim.

> [SEXTUS *is overpowered and bound.*

Now, Alpindargo, let thy men lead hence
This old man and his daughter. Till I claim
My captive, let them have a conduct safe
Unto a place of safety and a guard.
See that he touch her not, lest in his frenzy
He rob me of her as he would do now.
Give him his arms. Let him be treated well.

ALPINDARGO.

Ullin and Orla, take a guard of men
And bring this man and maiden to my cave,
And guard them safely there until I come.

> *Enter* THEUDAS *hastily.*

THEUDAS.

The prisoner is escaped. I found him not.

KALIPHILUS.

Fool! he is here. Go now prepare my ship.
Make all things ready; let the oarsmen be
Fast at their posts; then haste to let me know.
Thou 'lt find me waiting at the great oak-tree.
[*Exit* THEUDAS.

SEXTUS.

Farewell, Salome —

KALIPHILUS.

Hurry them away.

SALOME.

Oh stay. Oh, let me see him — but one moment —
[ANTONIUS *and* SALOME *are led out.*

ALPINDARGO.

Prepare the victim; let the rite proceed.
Already are the gods impatient.

CARACTACUS.

Stay!

A messenger!
Enter a MESSENGER.

MESSENGER.

The Romans are upon us!

They have surprised our sentinels, have forced
Our ramparts, slaughtered all our men, and now
Are swiftly marching for this place.

CARACTACUS.

And thou —
Wert thou one of the garrison?

MESSENGER.

I was.
And I alone escaped to˙ tell the news.

CARACTACUS.

Thou coward! Go and join thy comrades.

[*Stabs him.*

MESSENGER.

Oh!

[*Dies.*

KALIPHILUS.

I 'll go and seek my treasure, then aboard;
Leave here Antonius with this gentle hoard;
Teach sweet Salome how to be my wife,
To wander, and be cursed, like me, with life.

[*Exit* KALIPHILUS.

CARACTACUS.

Now, warriors, follow me; priests, do your work.
For, ere yon star shall wink its sleepy eye

The full of fifty times, we 'll bring you back
More victims than your altar-fires can burn.
On, warriors, to the fight! your war-cry be —
Briton and freedom! death or liberty!

[*Exit* CARACTACUS, *with* BARDS *and* WARRIORS.

Under a large Oak.

KALIPHILUS.

KALIPHILUS.

THERE moves the clanging, crashing march of
    Death.
Fools! How they groan and shriek beneath
    his tread!
When with impatient cry, and headlong rush
With music's cheer, they fling them in his track.
Now should they shout with very joy to know
That they can die, and that their tarrying's
    ended.

BARDS, *from the distant fight.*

Come, shades of mighty men,
Ye forms of heroes from dark vale and glen,
Where ye have fallen. Awful ghosts
Of bards in cloud-like hosts,
Who in the dreadful mountain chasms sigh,
Or, moving high,
Around their craggy summits cling,
Upraise your voices, sing
War's tempest song,
Roll it with shrieks along,

And let your harps primeval forests be,—
Your gong, the sea.

KALIPHILUS.

Now voice of harp and harper is borne down
In the deep surging fight, with curse and groan.
Howl, howl ye priests ; doubtless your gods
    will hear.

DRUIDS, *from the neighboring grove.*

Uplift thine arms,
Send swift alarms,
God of the mighty sledge.
Put up the shield,
Bow and quiver wield,
Sharpen the spear, and whet the axe's edge,
God of the battle.
Let loose the hurricane,
Tornadoes wild unchain,
With hail-storms rattle,
God of the wind.
Lead on the torrent's wrack,
Flame in the thunder's track,
Terror unbind,
God of the fiery breath.
To torture and to death
Our fierce invaders send,
That they no more may draw the sword, nor
    bend

The bow.
Pour on them torments and undying woe,
And whip them through the world of ghosts
    with rods
Prepared in council by ye all, ye gods.

KALIPHILUS.

To tarry, tarry, tarry till He come.
To walk, to walk, to walk until He come. —
Nay, Penitence, thy meek face taunteth me,
Thy sweet voice calleth jeering echoes up
From graves in valleys of mine ears, and back
From the long mountain ranges in my brain.
Ah! there are burdens which thou canst not
    lift
From the oppressèd soul. Away! begone!
I hate thee. Ay, to tarry till He come.
To walk, to walk, to walk! O God! no death.
When He shall come, what then? Then death?
    Then rest?
Insensibility? Oblivion?
Or larger life, and greater punishment?
Oh words inevitable in mine ears
Forever sounding, with a voice that shakes
My marrow, curdles all my blood, and lifts
My matted hair like rays above a cloud,
Cease, cease awhile, let my racked conscience
    rest.

Go faster, Jew; go faster. O great guilt
O'ertopping the huge daring of the Titans,
Or the impious mockery of Aaron's sons,
Or Heaven-defying pride upon the plains
Where Babel's tower, falling, bows its head,
I 'll glory in thee; be my pride my crown,
Than which the arch fiend himself can find no
      greater
To girt his mountain brows, as black clouds
      hang
Around the front of Sinai, or the top
Of heaven daring summits breathing fire.
He snatches at it vainly mad with envy.
Oh, were I tall enough to reach the heavens,
And in defiance wear it 'fore the throne! —

Enter THEUDAS.

Well, knave, what news? what news! Speak —
      speak, I say.

THEUDAS.

A body of the Romans have assailed
The sacred grove. Old Alpindargo 's slain.
Bernice and Thona fled aboard thy ship,
The druids captured, Sextus is set free,
And rages like a tempest long pent up,
Which breaks at length its bars —

KALIPHILUS.

Fool! is he armed?

THEUDAS.

Ay, armed; and when I saw him last he held
A trembling druid in his giant grasp;
With awful threats he bade him lead the way
To Alpindargo's cave, where, as thou knowest,
Salome waits.

KALIPHILUS.

But did he do it?

THEUDAS.

The druid?

KALIPHILUS.

Yea, knave.

THEUDAS.

He promised; and if terror take not
All his poor wits, he'll do it.

KALIPHILUS.

I must be there
Before him. But the ship?

THEUDAS.

All things are ready;
The oarsmen in their seats, the sails attend.

KALIPHILUS.

Keep all in readiness till I come there.

Alpindargo's Cave.

ANTONIUS, ULLIN, ORLA, AND SALOME.

ANTONIUS.

THE villains have withdrawn to rest awhile.
But we shall win, Salome, we shall win.
Oh, this is joy, in such a storm to find,
And from it save, my child.   Thou art twice
    mine.

SALOME.

All thine, a thousand times thine own, my
    father.

ULLIN.

Behold !   They will come on again.

ANTONIUS.

                           'T is well.

The father rages in me as a lion,
And hath the strength of twenty thousand
    youths.
Fear not, my love ; we 'll make them harmless
    ghosts.
Another kiss, my child — here, in my arms.

SALOME.

Ah, thou dost bleed! Art wounded?

ANTONIUS.

It is naught,
My gentle one. Thou art a warrior,
Thy father's child — a shade too pale, mayhap.
Thy silent courage is a hero's. Love,
Thou yet shalt be the brightest jewel in
The brightest crown e'er worn by regal Rome —
The crown in which her Roman matrons shine.

SALOME.

Ah! here they come again.

ANTONIUS.

Well, let them come.
I am refreshed. Another kiss, my girl.
So, stand thou now a little back.

SALOME.

Oh, no.
Let me be near thee.

ANTONIUS.

Nay, my child, stand back.
Come Valor, Vengeance, Hope, Despair, Hate,
Love, —
Come all and help me.

SALOME.

                    Let me hold thy shield
Before thee.

ANTONIUS.

Nay, brave girl, mine own, stand back.

ULLIN.

Now, comrade.

ORLA.

            I am at thy side, dear Ullin.

Enter TORSA, *the three* PIRATES, *and some* WARRIORS *assaulting.*

ANTONIUS, *fighting.*

Aha! ye caitiffs, — Now that I would live
With and for thee Salome — down, thou slave —
Youth flames again within me.

TORSA.

                    Cowards! dolts!
What! shall a dotard and two traitors hold
Ye here at bay? Think of the victors' spoils.
She's there, she's there within, the captive
        maid.

ULLIN.

Gods! but the curs are fierce! Be firm, good
        Orla.

ORLA.

To death, for them and thee, if need be, Ullin.

ANTONIUS. ·

See how they fall, Salome! Hope upholds
Its banners. Ah, good arm, thou 'st not forgot
Thy cunning, — to thy den in Hades, hound!

TORSA.

Have at them! Tear them down.

ULLIN.

Strike home, dear Orla.

ANTONIUS.

Death and the Furies seize thee. See! another,
For thee and me, Salome. See them fall!
To Tartarus and blackest torments rush,
Ye howling fiends! Give me thy thunders, Jove!
O Mars, Minerva! O Eumenides,
Pursue them.

ORLA.

Ullin, shall we sally forth
And drive them howling —

ULLIN.

Orla! Art thou hurt?

ORLA.

I 'm sped — this arrow — mind me not — farewell.

[*Dies.*

ULLIN.

A score shall pay me for thy single life,
My generous friend, too venturous, too brave.

SALOME.

Oh, there is Sextus! I can hear his voice!
O father, there is Sextus! Seest thou not
His armor gleaming in the moonbeams there?
Oh, he is saved! O father, he is saved!

SEXTUS, *without.*

Infernal blood-hounds, to your kennels! Ho!
Good heart, Antonius : good heart, my friend.

SALOME.

He moves a whirlwind. Roman soldiers now
Come on to join him.

ANTONIUS.

Ha! the knaves give back.

TORSA.

Thou liest. Now thou art mine.

ANTONIUS.

What! cur, so bold?

[*They fight,* ANTONIUS *is wounded.*

SALOME.

O father —

ANTONIUS.

Peace, my child.   Now, dog, to hell!

[*Runs him through.*

SEXTUS, *without.*

Hold fast, Antonius : we are with you straight.

ANTONIUS.

Ay, Sextus.   Ay, brave Sextus.

[*Falls.*

SALOME.

Thou art slain !

Enter KALIPHILUS *through a secret passage.*

KALIPHILUS.

Salome, come.

SALOME.

With thee ?   Oh, never !

ULLIN.

Hold !

SALOME.

O save me, Sextus! Father, Ullin, help !

ULLIN.

Thou shalt not touch this maiden.   Hold, I say.
Wert thou the god of hell I would withstand
thee.

KALIPHILUS.

Fool! wilt thou die? Then be it as thou wilt.
[*Stabs him.*

ULLIN.

Farewell, Salome.   I would still have lived
For thee — to fight — I die — alas! — too soon —
[*Dies.*

ROMAN SOLDIERS, *without.*

Ho! Victory!   The cowards flee!

SEXTUS, *without.*

Pursue.

SEXTUS *is borne in, wounded.*

SEXTUS.

Now leave me here, good friends: join the pursuit.
[KALIPHILUS *seizes* SALOME *in his arms.*

SALOME.

O Sextus, save me!

KALIPHILUS.

He's too late.   Ha, ha!
[*Exit* KALIPHILUS, *bearing* SALOME.

SEXTUS.

Ho! stay him!   Seize him!   Kill him!   Where
are ye?

All in that cursed pursuit. O gods ! O demons !
To lie here crippled by that villain's club !
Antonius ! What, art thou dead ?   Ye fiends !
But this should make a man curse all the gods,
And tempt his death from their swift indignation.
Ho, Soldiers ! Romans ! Help ! Can no one
      hear ?
Oh, but I will pursue him, by the gods !
And find him, though he hid in darkest Hades.

ANTONIUS.

Salome.

SEXTUS.

        Ah, thou livest !   'T is some good
In all this cursèd ill.

ANTONIUS.

        Come here, Salome.

SEXTUS.

'T is vain ! She is not here, Antonius.

ANTONIUS.

She is not here ! not here ! She is not here ?
What ! have I dreamed ?

SEXTUS.

      Nay. She was here, but is not.

ANTONIUS.

Was here, but is not? What? How meanest
thou?

SEXTUS.

That traitorous fiend, that foul Kaliphilus,
Hath borne her hence.

ANTONIUS.

Then is she lost for aye!
Oh, I have had enough of life, enough.
Part, part my soul, and as a giant shade
In cloudy semblance move: spit storms forever,
O'erwhelm the substance of the natural world,
And shake it into chaos. Let there be,
Through all the breadth and depth of air-filled
space,
One wrathful howling storm, and that be thou
And let the hollow caves of Erebus,
By thy loud bellowings shaken, overthrow
The star-capped pillars of the firmament
Till all rush roaring down in general wreck.

SEXTUS.

Nay, I will find her yet.

ANTONIUS.

Too late! Too late!
I ne'er shall see her more — no more — no
more.

SEXTUS.

Art thou much hurt?

ANTONIUS.

It will suffice to cure me.
Alas, alas! I know not where they 've placed
her.
Ah! I remember now. I killed her — so —
I stabbed her. Yea, well, it was better thus,
I could not let her be his slave, you know.

SEXTUS.

Oh, for a surgeon! For some one to help!

ANTONIUS.

My Livia, where hast thou placed the child?
Go, fetch her to the garden; let us play.

SEXTUS.

His wits unsettle. Have some mercy, gods.

ANTONIUS.

They 'd say that I am mad, but that were
false,
For madness is but weakness: I am strong.
Look at my falchion there; is 't not well
hacked?
Oh, I slew twenty of them, and their bones

Like dried twigs snapped. For all that I have
    learned
Naught goes so to the heart as a good thrust.

SEXTUS.

Will no one come? And must he die here
    thus?

ANTONIUS.

What! legs, have ye turned cowards, and refuse
To stand by me? For shame! we have been
    friends —
Perchance she 's hiding in the garden. Come.
She is so playful — when we find her out
You 'll hear her laugh — such music — it grows
    dark.

SEXTUS.

Oh, this is dreadful! Ho! What! Romans! Ho!

ANTONIUS.

I thought I heard her voice. Nay, art thou
    sure
She did not call me? I should know her voice.

ROMAN SOLDIERS, *without.*

Ho! call again. Where art thou?

SEXTUS.

        Here, within.

Enter some ROMAN SOLDIERS.

SEXTUS.

Run, fetch a surgeon ; here Antonius lies
At point of death. Be quick. How goes the
fight ?

A SOLDIER.

The isle is won, my lord. Caractacus
Is now our prisoner.

SEXTUS.

What is that chant ?

A SOLDIER.

The bards and druids marching to their death.
They are captives all ; and presently shall burn
Upon the altar piles they built for us.

ANTONIUS.

Search all the walks, — look under every bush,
The fairy rogue is teasing her. fond father —
Now, boy, gird on my sword ; my breastplate
now ;
Nay, not so close ; undo it still a little —
A little more — 't is tight here, at the throat.
My helmet — buckler — spear — I must away.
Give me my cloak, the night is growing cold.
The march may be a long one — let us go.

[*Dies.*

DRUIDS *without, chanting as they pass to execution.*

For death 's a tranquil lake, ne'er tossed, and
  never troubled.
The just are gently led there, the unjust
  dragged by terrors.
And thence, as mists arise, when summer days
  are dawning,
The souls of just men mount and move aloft
  to heaven ;
The unjust souls, as clouds, when wintry night
  approaches,
Are driven o'er the earth in storms, dark,
  writhing, roaring.
White are the misty robes of the just ;
Bright, in sight of the smiling gods,
As clouds which the smiling sun calls up
To rest in his glowing presence.
This light to glory turns their robes ;
Their forms are those of gods,
And halls of many colored air their dwelling.
But the unjust take the forms of ravenous
  beasts,
Flesh devouring birds, or of reptiles crawling.
Never come they to the gods' bright pres-
  ence, —
Moving always in the shades of night,
Caverns, fens, and slimy pits their home.

Therefore shall the just man not fear death,
    but seek it gladly;
Therefore will the unjust fear and flee, but
    vainly seek to shun it.

        [They pass from hearing.

THE END.